ALONG CAME
THE RAIN

Alison R. Solomon

Wild Girl Press

Copyright©2018 by Alison R. Solomon

Cover Design: Cindy Bamford
Copy Editor: Carol Vitelli

Published in the United States by Wild Girl Press

ISBN: 978-0-9984400-4-0

DEDICATION

To my wife, Carol, with my deepest love

And to all those struggling with memory issues

PROLOGUE

I know it was a drastic plan, but I had to do it. All those poor kids in foster care never ending up with permanent homes. All those people who run out of options when they have no money. The fear and anger were tearing at my insides, creating an intolerable vortex that threatened to pull me in, so I took the power into my own hands.

I had the perfect plan to create a win-win situation. Not only would it help the kids, it would help my personal situation as well. No harm to anyone. Everyone comes out ahead.

And then a couple of small glitches.

The next thing I know, I'm fighting for my life.

CHAPTER ONE

Wynn, June 22

It's raining when they arrest me. Not a light New England drizzle, but a heavy, Florida-summer downpour, the kind that creates puddles in seconds, and floods in minutes. As the two police officers hurry me out of the front door and down the drenched flagstone path, I have to keep myself from slipping on the wet ferns and sodden, scarlet hibiscus flowers scattered in the storm. Barker looks like she's in shock. She keeps repeating in a low voice, "I'll get you out of there," like a Buddhist mantra. Poor Barker. She must be beside herself with worry.

It all happens so quickly. One minute we're sitting in the living room, watching a rerun of one of our favorite episodes of *Friends* (the one where Ross finds his red sweater). The next, Barker answers the door to two uniformed police officers who tell her they need to take Wynn Larimer down to the station for questioning. I don't know who was more shocked—her or me. I could understand being arrested if I had committed a crime, or if I knew someone who had, or if I were connected in any way to any kind of criminal activity. I could comprehend it if I had a hidden past that had finally caught up with me, but I've been a model citizen from the time I was a straight-acting kindergarten teacher in my twenties to my current status as a middle-aged, suburban, jewelry-making lesbian.

"She's on Aricept," Barker yells at the officers as one of them pushes down on my head, shoving me into the patrol car. "It's very important she doesn't miss a dose." She thrusts a prescription bottle at the male cop but he holds his hand up and says he isn't allowed to take it. The young female one tells her to put it in my pocket. "She won't be able to keep it, but when they take her property, they'll have an accurate record of the dosage. If they keep her, they'll make sure she gets some, eventually."

My memory medication is the least of my worries right now.

The AC blows harshly on my wet legs and arms as I shiver in the back of the car, shaking out my dripping, limp curls. I try to get the attention of the cops, but there's a metal grill separating us and they have no intention of turning around. When we arrive at the police station, and they pull me out of the cruiser, I ask what I'm being charged with. The mean cop mumbles contemptuously, "Like you don't know," while the younger one says, with almost a hint of sadness in her tone, "It's not an arrest. We're detaining you. We don't have to bring any charges yet. But if we do, it will most likely be for false imprisonment." False imprisonment? *Isn't that what you're doing to me?* I want to ask, but it doesn't seem like a good idea. When I used to visit Mom in the nursing home, half the ladies there would tell me they'd been kidnapped and were now falsely imprisoned. I hardly want to sound like one of them. But I've never imprisoned anyone in my life. Why would they think I have? Who did I imprison?

The next part is a blur but I know it involves being photographed and fingerprinted and repeating my name and address several times. Then they tell me I'm going to a holding cell. I can barely bring my feet to move as a large-boned officer walks me down the corridor. We pass cells that have no doors, just metal grates from top to bottom, where you can see everything the women in the cells are doing: slouching on their cots, shitting on the toilet. A young woman in a red bustier, black leather shorts, and boots that come up to her thighs, yells, "What did the old lady do? Rob Medicare?" I'm offended that she thinks I'm old, but I feel grateful for my age when we stop at a cell that has a proper door, with just a small metal grate in it, that they can pass food through.

After the door clangs shut, I look around me. Mom would have described this cell as barely having room to swing a cat, and although I detest that expression, it's true. Two steps in one direction, three in the other and I'm at the perimeter of the cell. A foot away from me is the lower of two concrete slabs, each with a mattress so slim it would be more accurate to call it a yoga mat. The slabs are attached to the wall and narrow enough to preclude two cellmates lying together should they be so inclined. I ought to claim one of the bunks as mine, since it appears I may be here for a while, but my choice is between a rock and a hard place. The upper bunk involves climbing up a small ladder, but lately my balance is so bad, I don't think I should risk this. However, if I lower myself onto the other one, which is about knee-high,

I may not be able to stand up again. So for now, I perch on the stainless-steel toilet, which is awkward and extremely uncomfortable as it has no lid and the rim is cold and hard.

Sitting on the edge of this metal toilet, my whole body aches. I can feel the arthritis in my hips starting up and if I really have to sleep on that yoga mat, I won't be able to move by tomorrow morning. I want Barker. I want a lawyer. Nobody comes to get me, nobody interacts with me. As the hours wear on, I feel like I may go crazy in this cell, all by myself, with no one to talk to. It must be late evening by now. I thought they'd have had a detective ready to talk to me as soon as I got here, but perhaps they're trying to psych me out by making me wait. They want me to confess to something I didn't do. I've read about upright citizens who committed crimes with the Black Panthers or the Symbionese Liberation Army in their youth, who finally get caught when they're middle-aged, but I'm not one of them. (And yes, I get that Ms. Bustier and Black Boots might not categorize me as middle-aged, but when she gets to be my age, I guarantee she will no longer think of fifty-nine as old.)

I wonder what Barker's doing now. Did she walk the dogs? Of course she did. I'm the one who sometimes forgets, until I see them standing in front of me, their mournful eyes begging me to give their bladders some release. Did she heat up the curried vegetables I cooked earlier today for our dinner? Probably not. If she had any appetite she probably took a hot dog from the freezer, microwaved it, and slapped it on a bun with some ketchup. Hopefully, she's frantically calling anyone she can think of to get me out of this mess. She knows enough people in her line of work. One of them has to be able to help me.

I keep going back to that idea of false imprisonment. Who could I have imprisoned? The only people I know of who are kept somewhere against their will are either spouses—and clearly Barker's at home, so that's not it—or girls who go missing and are forced into sex work. Barker has two clients who are missing right now, fifteen-year-old foster kids who disappeared when they were being transferred from a foster home over a week ago. She's voiced her fear several times that they were abducted and are being kept somewhere. Could it be them? Do the police think I had something to do with their disappearance? That makes absolutely no sense. And yet they told me they had irrefutable evidence.

I know my memory's bad, but this is crazy. Surely I couldn't have done something like this and not remember? If I didn't do it, there's only one other option, the thought that went around and round in my head while I was shivering in the police cruiser.

Someone has set me up.

CHAPTER TWO

Barker, One Week Earlier

"Kallie and Michaela haven't shown up for tennis camp for two days. I've tried calling Mrs. Clark, the foster mother, but there's no answer."

Is it disapproval or concern I hear in the program director's voice? Either way I have to follow up. The girls' absence is surprising, but the lack of communication from Mrs. Clark is a bigger concern. She's one of my best foster mothers and she doesn't mess up.

I ease my green pickup truck into park in front of the Clark's sprawling ranch home and sit for a few more moments, unable to tear myself away from Terry Gross interviewing the first Iranian transgender politician on NPR's *Fresh Air*. How that woman consistently finds such interesting people to put on her show is beyond me. Although I love being on the road for my job, it's frustrating as hell when I arrive at my destination and have to turn off the radio in the middle of a good interview. In theory, I could listen later on the Internet or via a podcast, but I always forget. And the times I do remember, I get too distracted, knowing I could be washing dishes from dinner (my job; Wynn cooks), catching up on the never-ending pile of unfinished client paperwork, or taking the dogs out for a walk. Maybe today I'll remember to listen. Meanwhile, I shut off the car engine reluctantly and make my way to the front door. If I have to interrupt Terry, at least it's one of my favorite home visits.

When nobody answers the doorbell, I step back and walk around to the side of the house. The garage door is down so there's no way of knowing whether or not a car is parked behind it. Mrs. Clark has been a Pinellas County foster parent for four years and she's one I rely on a lot. We don't have many foster parents willing to take on teenagers, but she does a fantastic job with them. First she fostered Latoya and Kenya for a year till their birth dad won custody, then Bobbie and Chris, the adorable sisters who stayed with her for almost two years before they were claimed by a newly sober aunt. Now it's Kallie and Michaela, the troubled teens, though not as troubled as they used to be. Mrs. Clark is a natural; she gives them the parenting they need, and she also works really well with the county workers, willingly completing the ever-changing training and documentation requirements. Our scheduled appointment isn't until next week so I wasn't planning on coming out here today, but hopefully a quick visit will clear everything up.

I ring again, standing back to inhale the strong scent of gardenia from the bush by the door. Still no answer. I know I should try Mrs. Clark's cell phone but I'd really like to make the most of having this free hour, so I decide instead to go sit in the car, write up the evaluation I performed this morning, and best of all, listen to the end of *Fresh Air*.

A knock on the car window startles me. I turn the radio down and open the window.

"You lookin' for Ms. Clark?" The child is about ten, a neighbor kid, I presume.

"Sure. You know where she is?"

"On vacation. Left a couple of days ago. I feed Molly for her."

"Molly?"

"The cat. She's giving me $5 a day. I change her litter too. Pretty cool, huh?" The young girl smiles.

"Very," I concur. "But you probably shouldn't be telling strangers nobody's home."

Normally I would let my supervisor know that something's going on at this home, but I don't have one at the moment. Gracie retired in June and hasn't been replaced yet. Sam, her boss, intimated to me that I'm in the running. He said I'm the longest serving caseworker, and encouraged me not to do anything that might jeopardize a possible promotion. When I asked who I should check in with, he said I don't need to report to anyone for now. "If anything blows up, let me know. Otherwise just get on with your job. I trust you not to mess up," he told me when I caught him in the parking lot as he hurried to his large GMC Yukon. I could see his young grandson bouncing around impatiently as he waited to be whisked away to Cape Canaveral. Being a supervisor would be a big promotion, so I don't want Mrs. Clark, or anyone else, messing it up. I decide I better call her cell phone after all and tap out the numbers on my Android. A high-pitched tone accompanied by a digital voice tells me that this number is no longer in service.

A little knot begins to form in my stomach. Where has she gone? These two girls aren't just any foster kids. They've been my clients longer than any others, and if I'm honest, I have to admit they're my favorites. It didn't start out that way. The first time I met Kallie, I wondered if I had what it took to be a foster care social worker. It was my first job out of grad school. At my two student internships I'd worked with college kids who had eating disorders. I knew working in foster care would be different and when I accompanied Detective Gordon on my first ever drug raid, I knew I'd entered a whole new world. It was like something out of a movie: they busted the door down, literally stomping over the smashed shards of wood, weapons drawn. But the scene that greeted us wasn't dangerous, it was pitiful. The men Gordon was after had left hours before. In front of us two women lounged on a sagging, low-slung corduroy couch, their eyes glazed over, giggling, even as the cops told them to raise their hands. It was only after the women fell silent that I heard sniffing. That was when I saw Kallie, a torn T-shirt exposing her tummy, a dirty pink sandal on one of her feet. She was cowering in the corner of the room, clutching an armless Barbie. I walked slowly toward her and extended my arms, ready to give her a big bear hug.

"Hi, sweetie. I'm here to keep you safe." I smiled at the little girl encouragingly.

"I don't need you," she snarled. "Get away from me!"

I was disarmed, but I tried to sound calm and confident. "Your Mommy's gonna need to go away for a little while. I'll find you a nice place to stay until she comes back."

"No!" It was a low guttural scream and before I could stop her, Kallie flew across the room toward her mother. The strung-out woman held out her arms to the little girl who ran into them and folded herself as close as she could into her mother's body. The woman was practically skin and bones. Her cotton tank top was falling off her shoulders and her cutoff shorts were loose around her waist.

"Don't let them take you away!" the five-year-old screamed.

"I can't stop them, honey," the woman drawled as she pushed Kallie toward me. "But I'll be back. Go stay with whoever the lady finds for you. And wait for me."

That was ten years ago. Every time I think I've found Kallie a permanent home with parents who are willing to adopt her, Kallie's mom shows up to claim her. Usually she holds it together for a couple of months—once she even lasted eight—always just long enough to blow the placement. Finding good placements hasn't been easy, because Kallie's always been convinced that her mom would get clean, stop dating violent men, and turn her life around. I thought taking her to the adoption parties, would help her realize how much better her life would be if she let go of that hope. But whenever she attended them, she always hung back, which meant prospective parents ignored her and went to talk to the amenable kids—the ones who smiled and said what the desperate, childless couples wanted to hear. I never could get those would-be parents to understand that it was the kids who hung back who made the better placements. Kids who greet potential adopters like long-lost family feel absolutely no attachment to them and once the honeymoon wears off, they're often deeply troubled.

Michaela was one of those children. Even though her mom was in the picture, she was more than happy to try to get into a fost-adopt situation. She'd sidle up to every adult in the room, smiling coyly, willing them to talk to her. The first time I placed her with a friendly, well-meaning couple who'd made a conscious decision to adopt instead of having biological children, I hoped this was a Happily Ever After scenario. The Fords adored Michaela. I explained Attachment Disorder to them so they wouldn't be surprised at how she might veer between appearing so loving but acting in ways that might show a total lack of emotion. They were willing to overlook her stealing food from the fridge and hoarding it in her bedroom. They were willing to hold her when she tantrummed for hours at a time. But when she cut off the dog's tail ("he kept whacking me with it when it wagged,") they gave her back.

I didn't give up. Next, I placed her with the Ortegas, an overweight couple who'd been told they'd never be able to have a child. Lorna Ortega was thrilled to have a little girl who had the same black eyes and dark skin she had, the same thick hair snaking down her back. Michaela settled in and stopped hoarding food. When she put pepper in the cat's eyes to watch if it would sneeze, they carefully explained to her why she must never do it again. Her behavior improved and so did her school grades. I was ready to terminate parental rights with her mom and set an adoption date, and then I got the phone call.

"We're pregnant!" Lorna Ortega was laughing and crying at the same time.

"That's wonderful. Michaela will be thrilled to have a little sister." My excitement mirrored hers. I was genuinely excited for her.

"Yes, well, that's the thing. You know we love Michaela, but… but…" Lorna had started crying and her husband took the phone from her. "But we can't risk her being around a newborn," he said firmly.

When Mrs. Clark's home became available, I knew it was the ideal placement for Kallie and Michaela. The two had met several times at holiday parties the agency held, as well as at gatherings for prospective adoptive parents. By the time they were teenagers, they didn't bother mixing with the adults. They took the soda and snacks into a corner with them and played Angry Birds on their cell phones until everyone left. I used to watch them and it broke my heart.

Since they moved in with Mrs. Clark, things have definitely been on the upswing. She enrolled them in tennis lessons—tennis of all things! —which they love. Kallie has a natural talent and Michaela's not bad either. They spend hours practicing together and even started playing in some junior tournaments before school ended. Their grades are getting better and since Kallie's Mom is now in jail for at least eighteen months, Kallie's settled down too. More importantly than all of that, they really like Mrs. Clark. She's the right mix of loving and firm and they thrive on it. We were all devastated when Mr. Clark died suddenly, but the girls turned out to be a great comfort to Mrs. Clark.

I've been trying not to get my hopes up, since both girls steadfastly refuse to give up on their moms, just as much as their moms refuse to give up on them. Still, I can't help visualizing the adoption ceremony, the judge in his red robes, the girls standing on either side of Mrs. Clark, beaming. But this sudden absence is troubling. I thought we had all agreed on a plan for the summer. I'm worried for my own skin and I'm annoyed with Mrs. Clark for making an unapproved change.

I trust Mrs. Clark and don't want to make trouble for her or for myself, so I'll make some reassuring noises to the camp director and wait a little while before I report the absence, but I can't wait too long. "Please," I breathe. "Let them come home soon."

CHAPTER THREE

Kallie, Two days earlier

Today has to be one of the craziest days of my life.

It starts when Mrs. Clark gets off the phone and has a really peculiar look on her face. It's a mix of sadness and resignation, like she'd been expecting something to happen, but hoping it wouldn't.

"What's the matter?" I ask her, putting my hand awkwardly on her shoulder.

She turns toward me and gives me a big hug. "You have to start packing," she says in a strangled kind of voice.

"What?" I ask, and then I repeat it again, only this time it's a yell. "What are you talking about? Why?"

"I don't know. I don't understand. She just said you girls are leaving this morning."

"Why? Where are we going?"

"I don't know. She didn't say. She just said she's gonna be here in an hour." We're standing in the hallway. I'm still in my PJs and she's in her flowery short cotton robe, because it's summer vacation and no one has to be anywhere in a hurry.

"Who called? Barker?"

"No. Barker's away. But she said the order came from Barker. She's going to be here in an hour."

"What's her name?"

"I don't remember. I was in such a state."

"You're going to just let some stranger come and take us away?"

I'm shaking really badly. It's been a long road to get to where I am with Mrs. Clark. Contented, that's the word I'd have used up until three minutes ago. At first I wasn't sure how I felt about her; she seemed a bit too good to be true. She was the kind of mom you read about—making us cupcakes, teaching us what hobbies are, helping us with our homework. I kept waiting for the other shoe to drop. When it didn't, I started to relax and enjoy myself. For the first time in history, I started sleeping solidly at night, and found that with a decent night's sleep, I wasn't as dumb as I thought. I even started getting As for English and Spanish. I stopped holding Mrs. Clark at arm's length and I unpacked the backpack I've always kept, ready to leave at a moment's notice. Mrs. Clark started making little comments, implying she might even adopt me if my mom gave up her parental rights. Whenever she would say that I'd just kinda shrug. Agreeing to it seemed like it was a betrayal of Mom. But lately I've started thinking about how much Mom's betrayed me over the years. I started to imagine what it would be like to have Mrs. Clark as my mom, and it felt good. But one phone call and it's all over. The other shoe has dropped.

Just then, Mikki comes out of the bathroom, still wrapped in her fluffy bath towel, and sees us standing there, probably both pale-faced, me with my hands on my hips. She looks at us suspiciously and asks, "What's going on?"

"They're moving us," I tell her, my face twisted in a snarl. I'm so fucking tired of getting my hopes up, thinking life is good, and then discovering it's a pile of shit.

She drops her towel in shock, then quickly picks it up and covers herself. I tell her what we know, which isn't much, and we get dressed and begin the grim task of packing. We don't have that much—Mrs. Clark's been encouraging us to get rid of our old stuff and start out fresh with things she buys us. One suitcase each and our daypacks, and we're both packed. Mrs. Clark goes to the hall closet and pulls out our tennis rackets.

"Here," she says. "Don't forget these." She pushes them forward.

I can't help noticing she's awfully calm and dry-eyed. Stupidly I thought maybe she loved us a little. Stupidly I thought that if someone called and told her out of the blue that we had to leave, she would burst into tears and cry.

"Nah," I say, "I don't need that."

"Please," she says, and finally I see tears brimming in the corners of her eyes. "You're really good and you know how much tennis relieves your stress. Don't stop playing. Maybe you'll think of me when you win your first tournament."

I grimace, but I take the damn racket and Mikki follows suit. Mikki hasn't said much the whole time and I can't make out what she's feeling. I figure she must be having some of the same reactions I am.

It appears that while we were packing, Mrs. Clark whipped up our favorite Pillsbury biscuits. She puts them on a tray and offers them to us, and Mikki grabs two. I know if I take one I really will burst out crying, and there's no way I'm gonna give anyone the satisfaction of seeing that. So I shake my head and turn my back on her.

"I'll just wrap them in this napkin," she says. She unzips my daypack and puts them inside it. I haven't had breakfast yet and I hear my stomach growl, but I clench my teeth. Then the doorbell rings and a dark-skinned lady is standing on the threshold, holding up her county badge. "I'm Parminder," she says and ushers us out of the house, barely giving us time to hug Mrs. Clark, and into her silver Prius. I've never understood when social workers use the big county cars and when they use their own. Generally their own cars seem like they're for good things and the black county cars seem to be bad news. But today's news can't get any worse.

"Where are we going?" I ask as she pulls out of the driveway, and I wonder if I'll ever see the cute ranch house again, with its rambling pink bougainvillea over the door and the blue morning glories I planted under Mrs. Clark's guidance, climbing the gate.

"I'm dropping you off near the bus station. You'll be picked up from there."

"Who by?" Mikki finally speaks up, and her voice is so squeaky I realize she's trying really hard not to cry.

"It's a surprise."

I feel exhausted already, even though it's barely 9:30 a.m. so I just let her drive and don't say anything else. I look out the window and think to myself that if we're headed to the bus station, they're moving us far away. And that means a new school, which is about as unfair as you can get. When I started high school last year I thought it would be the last time I'd ever be the new kid. Now, once again, we'll be the outsiders. Earlier, I felt desperately sad. Now I'm just pissed off.

Parminder drops us off opposite the bus station. There's a bench on the side of the road and she suggests we sit there. "You'll be picked up soon," she says and drives off.

I turn to Mikki. Her head is down and she's not even bothering to play a game on her phone. Just looking forlorn and dejected.

"How much money you got?" I ask.

"Why?" She jerks her head up.

"We could get on a bus, and just go anywhere. Start over. Pretend we're eighteen."

I've got her attention now.

"Where would we go?"

"I dunno. Orlando? Miami? It's not like there's anything keeping us here. But we have to hurry—whoever it is, will be here soon."

"But where would we find a place to live? And how would we pay for it?"

"We'd get jobs. We could work in McDonald's. Or we could coach tennis. Mikki, think about it. We've never just been left like this—it's our big chance."

"Why don't we just see where they're sending us this time? Maybe it'll be as nice as Mrs. Clark's. If it's not, we could always just leave one day instead of going to school." She's twisting the handle of her suitcase back and forth and I know she can't make a quick decision like I could. She's always been timid.

"Every place we've lived, they put us on the school bus, they drive us places, they follow our every move and check up on us. What if the next foster mom is a total bitch? Aren't you tired of it?"

"I—I don't know." She pauses and I think maybe I can convince her after all. I figure rather than push my case, I'll let her think for a minute. She pulls out her wallet and just when I think she's gonna count her money to see how far we can get, a white Kia Soul pulls up and a woman rolls down the window and says, "I'm here to pick you up," and it's too late.

Parminder said whoever was meeting us was a surprise,

like it was someone we already knew, but I've never seen this woman before. She doesn't introduce herself, and at this point, I really don't care who she is. I figure she's the new foster mom, though this is never the way it happens. There's always been a social worker to make the introductions.

She puts our stuff in the trunk and we climb in the back of the car.

"Does one of you want to sit up front," she asks, "so I don't feel like a taxi driver?" But we both stay put. "You're going to have such a wonderful time." She puts the car into drive and takes off. "I'm so excited for you."

Not what I expect to hear.

"Yeah?" I ask sarcastically, "Where are we off to—Disney World?"

She laughs. "No. But I'd say staying at a beachfront condo, all expenses paid, isn't a bad second choice."

Mikki looks at me and I raise my eyebrows.

The woman continues talking. "I think it's so neat that you get to do this. I know how hard it must be when you—" She stops, cuts herself off midstream, like she's already said more than she's supposed to. "Let's just say, you got lucky. Most foster kids never get an opportunity like this. Pelican Beach is so beautiful."

I've heard of Pelican Beach, an upscale resort I'd never expect to set foot in. I can only remember being at the beach once. One of the times I lived with Mom between her rehab and jail stints, her boyfriend loaded us all in his pickup and we drove to this isolated beach where there were no buildings in sight. It was chilly but I was determined to wade in the water. I kept my hoodie pulled over my head as I rolled up my jeans. I turned around to wave at Mom, but she and the boyfriend had already lit up joints and right then I knew my days with her were numbered. The next foster home I went to was Mrs. Anderson, and when I asked her if we could go to the beach, she said that beaches were too dirty and we'd just track sand all over the house. Besides, there was no need, she said, because we had a perfectly good neighborhood pool for swimming.

I never heard of any foster parents living in swanky beach resorts and I still don't understand why we're being moved out of Mrs. Clark's, but my bad mood is definitely lifting. We drive the bridge across the Intracoastal and I see yachts bobbing, people kayaking, and fishermen in long waders casting their fishing rods. We turn onto a wide boulevard, lined with luxury high-rises and large, gated-building complexes. It feels like a different world from the ranch bungalows and chain-link fences of Pinellas Park.

She pulls up in front of one of the buildings. Not quite as luxurious as the ones we passed. There's no security guards, or intercoms or glass entrances, but it's still pretty amazing and it leads right onto the beach.

As we get in the elevator, she tells us, "You deserve this. It's going to be an experience you'll never forget."

She tells us that we're going to be staying in an apartment that's just for the two of us.

"I can't believe it," I tell her. "No one ever let us be unaccompanied. There's always someone telling us what to do or when to do it." I can't even imagine what it's like to have no adult supervision.

"I'm sure you girls can handle it."

Of course we can. You don't get to be in foster care for ten years without becoming pretty independent. I can keep house. Heck, some of the places I lived in had me doing that when I was barely big enough to hold a broom. I know how to get myself up in the morning, how to shop for bargains and manage money, even though I've hardly ever had any. For my entire fifteen years every time I've wanted to do something, or buy something, adults have told me, "You can do that when you're older," or, "When you're living on your own, then you can do that." Well guess what? That time is now!

I don't notice what button she presses in the elevator, but it must be pretty high because I feel my stomach flip when we whoosh upward. The corridor leading to the condo is carpeted with thick, red pile. When we reach the condo, an end unit, it's unlocked. We walk through the front door and she leads us into a small living room that has a sofa, love seat, standing lamp and not much else. But what draws me in is what I can see beyond the living room. I move towards the floor-to-ceiling windows and look out at the entire Pelican Bay laid out in front of me. Far below, the gulf shimmers in the sun and I can't believe I'm going to stay in an apartment that has a view this spectacular. Who's paying for this? I want to ask, but I don't, because clearly everything is under her control and I'm not going to worry about it.

We walk past the living room and a small dining nook into the kitchen. She opens the pantry and I see it's stocked with enough food for a week: Cheerios, Pop-Tarts and Little Debby's; ramen noodles and spaghetti; pork and beans, chicken soup and Spam. Then she shows us the pizzas and ice cream in the freezer, and I catch sight of some beer bottles in the refrigerator. I wonder if they're for us, but decide not to push my luck and ask. Perhaps she didn't notice they were there. Or perhaps they're for someone else. But I make a mental note to grab one the moment she leaves. Mikki turns to the fruit bowl on the countertop and can't stop herself from taking a banana.

"What's the catch?" Mikki asks as she pulls back the peel.

"There is no catch," she replies. "You deserve it." And it's true. Mikki and I have been through more than most kids our age. It's time we got a break.

"Where's the bedroom?" I ask and she corrects me.

"Bedrooms" she emphasizes the "s." "You each have your own."

We go back down the hall and she points Mikki toward one door and me the other. I open it and the first thing I see is a large queen-sized bed. I can't believe it. Up until now, I've only ever slept in a single bed. And most of the time I had to share a room too, often with kids half my age. That pretty much sucked, except for when I shared a room with Shawna at Miss Cooper's. The second week Shawna was there, she got her period for the very first time. She had no idea what it was. I explained everything and made her tell Miss Cooper, who gave her a large packet of Always and told her she couldn't use tampons until she was older. Crap, I told her, and demonstrated up close and personal just how to use them. She struggled a bit, but I showed her how to relax the same way one of mom's many boyfriends showed me. After Shawna and I practiced putting tampons in a few times, we were best buds. So then I taught her how to shoplift candy from the Mexican grocery store on the corner. But the bitch told another of the kids in the home and I was out, moved back to Summerhill with all the new kids and losers till they got me a placement with Mrs. Anderson and her family. That's a story for another time. Suffice it to say, I look around this apartment and think, my own room *and* my own bed? Priceless.

Apart from being just for one person, the bedroom is

nothing like any of the foster homes I've been in, good or bad. No shiny Disney princess wallpaper or peeling paint on the walls, no new stuffed animals or ratty teddy bears on the pillow, no new toys on a shelf or broken dolls shoved in a corner, no comics or books, no desk for doing homework. The bed has a plush red satin quilt which matches the scarlet curtains with creamy valances hanging over the windows. There's a dark wood vanity with a little cushioned stool facing a large framed mirror. I walk inside the room and see a little door leading off it and when I peek through I see a toilet, a sink—and there's even a tub! My own bathroom? Are you kidding me? No more sharing with dirty little kids who leave the lid off the toothpaste so there's white goop everywhere, and who leave dirt stains on the washbasin? No more waiting behind a locked door with my legs crossed while some kid says he's taking a piss but is actually gorging himself on food he hid in there?

I go back to the hallway beside myself with glee.

"Welcome to your summer vacation," she says to us both. She turns around and I see a man standing in the hallway who I swear wasn't there before. "I want you to meet a friend of mine," she says. He's older than us, but not old. Small goatee, wire-rimmed glasses, tailored suit. He looks cool, like someone I wouldn't mind hooking up with. Not that I'd ever get someone as distinguished looking as him. But I decide to be bold anyway, and stepping toward him, I hold out my hand.

"Hi," I say. "I'm Kallie. What's your name?"

He looks startled, then a lazy smile appears on his face. "John," he says. "I guess you can call me John."

And he smiles, like he's making some kind of joke.

THREE MONTHS
EARLIER

CHAPTER FOUR

Wynn, March 1

I must be on time tonight. We're meeting Dot and Evie for dinner and last time I was an hour late. Barker tried really hard not to get mad at me, but I could tell she was embarrassed. The waiter wouldn't seat them at their reserved table until everyone was there, so they had to sit at the bar, drinking cocktails. By the time I arrived, the high barstools had put Dot's back out of whack and she spent the rest of the evening writhing and fidgeting in her chair like one of the kindergarten kids I used to teach. I apologized profusely and of course, they were gracious, but tonight I will be on time.

I like Dot and Evie, but I admit they intimidate me. Dot has a high-powered job in a financial services institution doing something with information technology. I've asked her a number of times what she does, but I never seem to quite understand the answer. I know she makes a lot of money. Evie is a massage therapist and the reason she intimidates me is that she's absolutely drop-dead gorgeous. I never believed in the whole butch/femme thing until I met them. We were at a fundraiser for the counseling agency Barker used to work at and in walked this distinguished-looking couple. I thought they were straight until I looked closer and saw that the guy in the tux and bow tie was actually not a dude at all. Evie was wearing stilettos, a sequined black cocktail dress that hugged her hips, and her cleavage put all of us to shame. You could see it was all her, with "all" being the operative word.

Dot and Evie like to eat at the kind of upscale restaurant I thought existed only on TV and they think nothing of dropping a couple hundred dollars for a meal. After we became friends, they insisted we let them pay when we went out for dinner, since they knew we couldn't afford those kinds of prices. It still makes me uncomfortable but Barker assures me it's nothing to them. From time to time, we invite them to our home for dinner. I cook elaborate meals, and they gush over the food, though in truth, I'm not sure if they really like it. Evie pushes the food around and takes a couple of bites, declaring it "heavenly," or "divine," and Dot shovels it in as fast as she can without seeming to pay any attention to what it is. They do the same thing when we eat out though, so I guess I shouldn't take it personally.

Four thirty. I put down the thread I've been stringing beads on. I replace the beads in their container and line up the variety of tools and implements I use to make my necklaces. Barker thinks I ought to put them away, but if I did, I'd never remember where I put them, and I'd waste too much time just trying to find them again. I'm careful not to drop any of the beads because picking them up is a task that can take hours. I take one last look, assure myself that everything is tidied away in its place, then close the door behind me. In the bedroom, I rifle through the closet trying to decide what to wear. We're doing Indian food tonight. Even though I seem to have a somewhat sensitive stomach, I love curry. It loves me too—my blouses and pants especially. I don't know that I've ever succeeded in eating curry without spilling at least a drop of it somewhere, and it stains instantly. So I forego the pink silk shirt (which Barker says is so dated I ought to throw it out) and instead go for a multicolored pant set that I hope will hide any stain that happens to find its way on there. The pants are looser than the last time I wore them and drag a little on the ground so I can't wear my beloved Tevas. I opt instead for a pair of ropey sandals that have a three-inch platform heel. I apply eyeliner and the new lip gloss Barker gave me ("That plum color will accentuate your gorgeous lips!" she said winningly) and look at the clock. Five fifteen. Plenty of time to make it by six.

When they see I'm getting ready to leave, our two dogs,

Queen and Latifah, jump off the sofa and come running over. Queen jumps up, putting her Miniature Schnauzer front paws on my pants and I push her off quickly. That's when I realize they need to be walked. I was so immersed in the necklaces, that I didn't take my usual three o'clock break to run them around the block. I debate changing back into my shorts and T-shirt, but figure it will take too much time, so I quickly leash them up and run outside.

We take off down the street and almost immediately, Queen has to stop and sniff a particular groove in the sidewalk. Our neighborhood association has strict rules about where the girls can relieve themselves and the sidewalk isn't one of those places. "Come on." I yank on her leash. "Let's run to the grass!" Latifah hears the word "run" and takes off with a Labrador leap. "Wait!" I yell, but she takes no notice, and yanks so hard that I feel split in two between Latifah going in one direction and Queen digging in her paws on the sidewalk. The situation is resolved when Public Enemy Number Three—a nasty little mastiff who baits Queen at every opportunity he gets—shows up across the street and both dogs turn in his direction, barking furiously, ready to attack. In less time than it takes to yell, "Stay!" my left foot is skidding off the three-inch platform heel, while my butt heads for the grass verge. Latifah glances back and cocks her head to one side as if to ask why I'm sitting on the ground, but Queen plows on, stopping only when I yank so tightly on her leash that she almost chokes. I pull myself up and look sternly at the dogs.

"Pee," I command in my best alpha voice. "Now!"

Both animals look contrite and do their business quickly. I hobble back indoors. My sandal is unwearable. I rush into the bedroom and find the only other pair of heels I own. They're black winter shoes, but hopefully no one will notice underneath the wide-hemmed pants. I shove my feet in them, and head out the door. If I drive really fast, I can still make it on time.

***

Amazingly, I find a parking spot just half a block from the restaurant. I hurry down the street, aware that I'm sweating rather profusely, but relieved that my watch registers 5:58 pm. Perfect. I enter the restaurant and look around. I'm the first one there. The waiter offers me a table and I explain that it's for four. He seats me and I order a glass of red wine. I sit so I can watch everyone entering and leaving. I'm shocked by how many gorgeous, petite, attractive young women seem to pair up with pot-bellied, short, balding older men. They cling onto their partners' arms as if they couldn't take a step without them, and the men march in looking prouder than the guy who just won the U.S. Open. I look at my watch and discover it's already 6:15. Panic starts to set in. Am I in the right place? This is one of those times when I understand why Barker thinks I should have a cell phone. I've resisted having one, just as I've resisted using the computer, beyond sending email and doing a few other basic things. Call me kooky but I'm just not ready to be a slave to technology. Still, if I had a phone now, I could call her and find out what's going on.

I drain my glass and the waiter is at my side asking if I want another. I don't really, but I can't just sit here, so I nod affirmatively. The couple next to me is having a heated discussion and I can picture Barker and me doing the same thing if it turns out I'm in the wrong place. I wrack my brain trying to remember if I've missed something. I distinctly remember last month at the sushi restaurant Dot saying we had to go Indian. I'm almost positive Evie suggested Bombay Queen, and I could swear that the last thing Barker said as she left this morning was, "See you at six." (And of course she added, "don't be late.") It's 6:45 and I suddenly realize that even though I don't have a cell phone, the restaurant must have a phone I could use. I ask the waiter and he points me to the bar in the back of the restaurant, where I grab the phone and dial Barker. It goes straight to voicemail. In a surprising moment of clarity, I remember Dot's number and quickly dial it.

I hear the phone pick up but it's so noisy I can barely make out what she's saying.

"Dot, it's Wynn."

"Where are you?"

My heart sinks. Clearly, I'm not in the right place. "Bombay Queen." She says something but I can't make it out. "I'm at the bar, it's noisy," I tell her. "Hold on."

I wonder where I can go and as I look around me, I feel a hand on my back. I whirl around so fast I almost smash into Evie's ample bosom. She laughs, but I'm already a wreck. I put the phone down and we walk back into the main room of the restaurant. Dot is perusing the menu and Barker is just walking in. They've taken a corner booth and since I left my wine glass at the other table, I have to tell them I've been there since six.

"But we agreed on 7:00, didn't we?" Dot looks quizzically at Barker.

"Yes. Don't you remember, Wynn, last thing I said as I left—see you at seven?"

"I…I thought you said six."

Barker glances at the other two and raises her eyebrows. "Don't worry about it, honey. Go get your drink and come sit down and relax." I turn around to go fetch my glass but Barker calls me back. "What on earth happened to your pants?"

"What do you mean?" My head is swimming a little from two glasses of wine on an empty stomach, I'm embarrassed that yet again I messed up, and I'm nervous because being with Dot and Evie always puts me on edge.

"You have an awfully large stain on your butt," Barker whispers. Dot and Evie both look up from their menus and I can see they heard what she said. I can't figure out what Barker's talking about until I remember Public Enemy Number Three. I was so busy changing my shoes, it didn't occur to me to check out my backside. I see the three of them exchange glances but Barker stands up and gives me a big hug.

"Honey, you look good, whatever you're wearing." she says, "I'm just happy to see you. It was a long day." She squeezes my butt and kisses me full on the mouth. That girl. She can make it so nothing matters. Her heart is so big it would melt Alaska. I hug her gratefully and hope she won't notice my winter shoes. Maybe the evening isn't ruined after all.

CHAPTER FIVE

Barker, March 15

We're driving up to Cedar Key, a funky little town on the coast, so Wynn can check out the Spring Arts Festival. They have a juried art contest and since Wynn has her sights set on entering an art show in St. Petersburg this summer, she wants to gather information. Her hope is to see what kinds of jewelry get accepted into the contest and which pieces win. I'm happy to go because Cedar Key is one of our favorite places. Natives call it "old Florida" and it's so laid back, you feel as if you're traveling back in time, to a fishing village where life was simple and people didn't abandon their kids and shoot up their veins.

Not that I'm naïve enough to think that doesn't happen in rural, sleepy, picturesque towns. I know bad stuff happens everywhere, and that sometimes the places which have the fewest diversions to offer their residents are the breeding grounds for teens and young adults to start their careers in addiction and drugs. But sometimes I like to forget all that, and just walk down the sleepy streets of small-town Florida and make believe life is the way it appears to be on the surface.

We usually visit Cedar Key in the height of summer when it's so hot only die-hard Floridians would choose to vacation here. We take kayaks out into the bayou, floating through the mangroves early in the morning as the sun rises. When we're lucky we see roseate spoonbills wading in the shallow waters, sweeping their paddle-like bills from side to side to sift up shrimp and mollusks, their pink wings flaming. You can always tell who's new to town when you overhear them on their cell phones telling their friends about the flamingos they saw; flamingos would never make it this far north. After we kayak, we go to one of the fish restaurants on the bay and buy enormous grouper sandwiches that last us all day. We nap in the afternoons and then take slow strolls through the sleepy town in the evenings.

But today there's nothing sleepy about Cedar Key. There must be over a hundred booths lining the main street. The weather is perfect: sunny and warm with a very slight breeze, ideal for strolling through an art exhibit and that's exactly what thousands of people are doing. The artwork is incredible—gorgeous pieces of sculpted glass, carved wooden statues, ceramic bowls, incredible watercolors, oil paintings and photographs, and of course, lots of jewelry. Wynn is as happy as a puppy with a new chew toy. Despite her arthritis, she darts back and forth from booth to booth, picking items up, examining them, asking questions, and talking to the artists. How do they decide what piece or pieces to enter into the competition? How much inventory would she need to have her own booth? How long does it take them to prepare for an event like this? Many of them sound like they're almost permanently on the road, traveling from one art show to another. Others are regional artists who have pieces in the local galleries and never venture outside Cedar Key. While Wynn engages them, I wander off on my own, eventually finding a little café where I order a white chocolate latte with whipped cream and enjoy my own little piece of heaven.

By the end of the afternoon, Wynn is ready to call it quits. I ask her if she wants to have dinner here but it's so crowded we both agree we'd rather find a place on the road.

"Let's go to Pelican Beach," she suggests as we head back south.

"Sure," I say, turning off the main freeway to take the coast road home. As we drive along the gulf, the small homes that line the gulf beaches turn into larger houses which, as we enter Pelican Beach, turn into massive condo buildings obscuring the gulf altogether as they sit like Monopoly hotels bunched onto Park Place.

"You wouldn't even know there were beaches behind all

those condos," says Wynn, her expression one of dismay. "Now I know why we've never been here before."

I'm startled. "Yes we have. Don't you remember? We came here when your mom visited us before she died." Sometimes Wynn shocks me. How can she not remember that?

"We did?"

My heart sinks. This is what it was like when her mom, Viv, was first diagnosed with Alzheimer's. We'd go visit her and talk about things we'd done in the past, and she'd look at us and say, "Did we? I don't remember that." At the beginning she'd get belligerent— "you're making it up, we never did that"—but when it got really bad, she stopped arguing and then it was even sadder because she didn't seem to mind that she couldn't remember anything. She'd ask about Wynn's father and when we said, "You got divorced when Wynn was a teenager," she'd say, "Really? Did I?" I dread that this is how Wynn is going to end up. Especially since she's so young. Her mom was in her eighties when she got like that. Wynn is barely sixty.

We park on the main drag, and go to a Cuban restaurant in a small shopping center. I purposely choose not to go to the restaurant we went to with her mom, because if I ask her if she remembers it, I'm not sure I want to hear the answer.

"I'm definitely going to do the art show," Wynn gushes. "The folks in Cedar Key were so helpful, and I got business cards from several of them who said they'd be happy to talk more on the phone."

"I'm glad it was such a successful trip," I take a large forkful of my Lechon Asado and revel in the mixture of spices that make it one of the best I've had in ages. I can taste the garlic and oregano, but there's something else that's making the pork melt in my mouth. "You have to make this for our next date night," I tell Wynn. "It's out of this world."

The fact that Wynn blanked out on having visited Pelican Beach is still weighing on me as we sit and eat. I wonder whether she purposely tries not to remember places that might be associated with her mom.

"Do you miss your mom?" I ask her. "Do you think about Viv much?"

It's been almost two years since she died. When I first met Viv, I couldn't get over how vibrant and energetic she was. She loved anything that had to do with the water. We took her on a dolphin trip and parasailing and then she decided she wanted to snuba. We didn't even know what that was.

"I saw it on TV," she told us. "It's a mix of snorkeling and scuba diving." She explained how you go deep down into the water like a diver, but instead of having an oxygen tank, you're attached to the boat up above by a long hose. I thought it sounded scary and Wynn couldn't do it because of her asthma. But Viv was determined, so on her next visit, we drove down the Florida Keys to Marathon, the closest place that had snuba diving. Wynn and I lounged at a nearby resort that had an infinity pool from which you could order drinks. When we picked Viv up four hours later, I'd never seen her so elated.

"Best adventure ever!" she announced. Four years later, she was still showing everyone the pictures she'd taken with her underwater camera: white coral, multicolored angelfish, spiny lobsters, and dozens of tropical fish whose names we didn't even know. Eight years later when we pulled out the photo album and looked at the pictures, she said, "That's pretty. What is it?"

For over a year Wynn drove back and forth to her mom, who lived about three hours away. She'd leave our house on Tuesday morning and come back Wednesday evening. Everything fell on her because she was an only child. She'd take Viv to appointments, buy her groceries, and clean her apartment. Occasionally we'd go on the weekend, so I could accompany her. It was easier for me to see how much she was deteriorating: the same questions asked repeatedly, the decreasing ability to cook and bake, the endless demands to search for things like her keys that turned up in the freezer or the oven. When it became clear that she could no longer live alone, Wynn suggested we bring her to live with us.

"I know you mean well, but I saw what it was like with my grandfather. He ended up incontinent, unable to feed himself, even forgetting how to talk."

"Viv's not going to get like that," Wynn said, but we both knew she couldn't be sure. We talked about it for weeks and eventually our decision was made for us. A social worker from the local hospital called to tell us Viv had broken her hip after she fell while wandering in the street in her pajamas and slippers. From the hospital, she went to a nursing home to rehab her hip.

After that it was clear that we should move her to the

dementia wing of that same nursing home. Unfortunately, it was a private place that cost a fortune and Viv had almost no money, but we couldn't move her anywhere else at that point. That's why I worry so much about Wynn. If she ends up needing care like that, there's no way we could afford it. But I know it's my responsibility to ensure that she gets whatever she needs and I'll do whatever it takes to make that happen.

"When I think of Viv," says Wynn, "I try to remember her before she went downhill. I picture us camping at Yosemite when I was a child, and traveling through Europe together when I was in my twenties. I miss who she was when she used to visit us here, but I don't miss who she became before she died."

We finish our dinner and head out of the restaurant. On the way home, I wonder to myself, will that ever be me? Telling people I miss Wynn when she was cooking complicated dinners for us on date night, and creating unique jewelry? That I miss the Wynn who kept up with politics and had strong opinions about them? I shake off the thought, reminding myself that's not where she's at. I'll just keep a really close eye on her for now, and something will work out.

CHAPTER SIX

Wynn, April 2

I definitely overextended myself today, although part of it isn't not my fault. Today is the last day to submit a curriculum for a jewelry-making class I'm teaching next month. I have a necklace that Evie commissioned as a surprise birthday gift for Dot. She wants to pick it up this evening, so she can give it to her tomorrow morning. Then they'll both come here tomorrow evening for dinner. That's the part that's not my fault. I was hoping we'd go to a restaurant, but yesterday Barker came home and presented me with all the ingredients I need to make mole poblano, which we've talked about me trying ever since we visited Oaxaca.

"I had a home visit near that massive Mexican supermarket, so it was the perfect opportunity to get all those seeds and spices you need for it," she said as she dumped well over a dozen little packages on the table. There were four different types of dried chilies, as well as tomatillos, peppercorns, cloves, coriander and anise. I kept opening the tiny packets which she'd carefully labeled, amazed how many ingredients one dish demanded.

The secret to a great mole is using everything when it's fresh, so that's why I need to cook today. I just wish she'd waited until tomorrow to buy it. I'd like to back out of cooking for them, but I know sometimes Barker feels a little resentful that I get to stay home all day while she's traipsing all over the county, dealing with difficult people who exhaust her. Also, I have no one to blame but myself that I didn't prepare the jewelry class weeks ago, and that I left it to the last minute to work on Evie's necklace.

I read through the recipe so I can work out how long I need to get everything done. I try to figure out whether I need to do some of the prep work in advance, before starting my crafting, or whether I can do what I usually do: work in my studio, which is upstairs at the back of the house, for several hours, and then stop, come downstairs, and throw myself into the cooking. I decide to do the latter, because the recipe looks complicated and once I start with it, I won't be able to stop in the middle.

Soon I'm immersed in hand-cutting silver that I'm forming into a monogrammed necklace. I want the D to swirl around the A of her last name. It's painstaking work but I love doing it. One of these days I'll buy a laser cutter, but for now, I enjoy using my simple tools. I complete the letters and am just melding them to the filigree chain, when Queen jumps up and pushes the tool in my hand so that it almost cuts right through the silver. I push her off and go back to my work. When I put the finishing touches to it, I can't help admiring how beautifully it flows. Dot will love it. I wrap it carefully in tissue paper and put it in a little white box.

I ought to take the dogs for a long walk but I decide to wait and take them before I start on dinner. I still have to prepare my class, and I want to make it perfect since it's the first time I've ever taught anything. It came about after I got talking to a young man who works at the community center in North County, when he came over to my stall at the Tuesday morning market. He asked if I'd be willing to teach a class. I didn't really want to do it, but I couldn't think how to say no politely. I was hoping no one would sign up but a couple of weeks ago he let me know the class was on, though I don't know how many people will attend, and I have no idea what level they'll be at. That's why I figured wire wrapping was a good idea. You don't need many tools and it's good for beginners as well as people who've created jewelry before. When I finally finish up the syllabus, I put my tools away, and close the door.

It's a lot later than I thought it would be, but now I can turn my full attention to the chicken mole recipe. I poach the chicken then shred it off the bones. I dry-roast the chili peppers, admiring the reds and oranges as they blister and change color. The recipe tells me to toast the peppercorns, cloves, cinnamon, coriander, and anise seeds until they're fragrant which seems a bit disingenuous; with a mix like that, they're fragrant the moment I take them out of their little packages. I fry up the raisins, almonds and pumpkin seeds and start humming, feeling heady with all the delicious aromas I'm creating. When everything is roasted and fried, I put it all in the food processor with a little water, until I have a smooth paste. I get out the Dutch oven and put it on the flame with some canola oil. Just then I hear Barker's key in the lock.

"Hi honey," I call out. "I'm in the kitchen!"

"Can you come help me out here?" she calls back, so I head to the front door, where I see she's carrying a large bouquet of sunflowers, along with an oversized bottle of Chianti.

"You're really making a date of it!" I smile and she looks puzzled.

"You do remember that Dot and Evie are coming for dinner, don't you?"

Now it's my turn to look puzzled. "I thought we were getting together with them tomorrow? Isn't tonight our date night?"

"Well yes," she answers and I can hear that she's trying not to get into a huff. "But they couldn't make it tomorrow because Evie's taking Dot to Orlando for a long weekend, so we agreed they'd come over tonight. Please tell me you finished her necklace?" I can hear her huff starting to build, but I nip it in the bud.

"Yup!" I say proudly. "And it looks spectacular." Then I smell the oil burning in the kitchen. I grab the bottle from her and rush into the kitchen, averting disaster. I empty the pan and pour fresh oil in the Dutch oven.

Barker follows me into the kitchen and heads to the sink with the flowers.

"I guess that means the table isn't set yet?" she sighs.

"No, but as soon as I finish with dinner, I'll set it. You go sit down and catch up with *Days of Our Lives*." It's the one anomaly that I could never get over, a woman like Barker wanting to follow that soap opera. But it's her way to unwind and it's fine by me.

A moment later, she's back in the kitchen, looking furious and grabbing paper towels.

"Didn't you take the dogs out? One of them peed on the rug in the living room."

Darn. I meant to take them before I started cooking.

"I'll put their leashes on." I try to soothe her.

"Don't bother. I know you still need to finish up. Come on girls!" she calls to Queen and Latifah and they come running gratefully.

I finish making the sauce and then let it simmer, while I go set the table. I clean myself up, then add the final ingredient to the mole—the chocolate. I dip a teaspoon into the sauce and run my tongue over the rim. Though I say so myself, the dish is out of this world.

***

For once even Evie does more than just push her food around.

"This is fantastic, Wynn, thanks so much!" It's a high compliment indeed.

"Mmm," says Dot as she scrapes her plate clean, "one of the best things you've ever made."

The evening has gone really well. We've almost finished the Chianti and everyone seems relaxed.

"Evie has something for you," says Barker, and retrieves the little white box from the credenza. She hands it to Evie, who hands it to Dot, who unwraps it, looks delighted, then frowns, and holds it up for all to see. Barker and Evie have the same reaction Dot did. At first they gasp with pleasure but then Evie looks embarrassed and Barker looks annoyed.

"What's the matter?" I venture, "You don't like it?"

"I love it," says Dot. "It's beautiful."

"Yes, but I can see there's something wrong with it." The three of them look at each other, then Barker speaks.

"Honey, don't you remember that Dot changed her last name when they got married in New York last year?"

Instantly I feel terrible. I completely forgot, but that was partly because they kept the whole wedding thing so low-key. It's still not legal in Florida and they said when it's legalized nationwide, then they'll have a big party.

"It's all right," Dot says quickly. "It was the thought that counts."

***

After they leave, I go into the kitchen and start on the dishes.

"Leave that, honey," Barker comes up behind me and puts her arm around my waist. "Come sit with me. You can do that tomorrow morning." I don't usually like to leave dishes in the sink, but quite often Barker is so tired, it makes a nice change to be invited to sit with her in the late evening.

While I dry my hands, Barker puts a scoop of banana pecan ice cream into a bowl for each of us. We sit close together on our new leather sofa.

"I want to talk to you about something," she says. My heart sinks. Having "a talk" never bodes well. But Barker pre-empts me. "It's nothing bad," she says, smiling. "I'm thinking about doing a spiritual retreat this summer."

She's taken me by surprise. Barker's one of those people who think a yoga class is too woo-woo for her. She's isn't religious, and the most spiritual she ever gets is when she says, "If there is a God, she's there, in that setting sun," when we take a late evening stroll along the beach. She scoffs when I try to teach her about the importance of balancing her chakras and she thinks crystals are for hippies.

"Sam suggested it." Ah, that explains it. Sam is her supervisor at work and she adores him. "He thinks I'm getting stressed out."

"You've always told me that was the nature of your job." I decide to play devil's advocate.

"It is. And I don't think I'm any more stressed out than usual, but…"

"Of course you have to go. Where and when?"

"It's in June, and they hold it in some very beautiful, very remote place in the middle of the state. Apparently it's quite luxurious, like a five-star hotel."

"Will the county pay for it?"

Barker laughs. "Knowing the county and social work budgets, do you think that's likely?"

It was a long shot, but after all, they're suggesting she go.

37

"Is it very expensive? Can we afford it?"

"It's pricey, but I ran the numbers and I don't think it would be a problem."

Barker is in charge of our finances. We both know it's her strong point and that I'm fairly clueless about money. I have a separate account for my business so that it's easier when we file taxes, but even that is something she stays on top of. I just put the money in the ATM and let her do the rest.

"Well then, you must go. It's only a few days and I can always call if I need something."

"Actually, you can't. They make guests unplug entirely— no TV, no Internet, and no cell phones. I think that's why people relax so much, though the gourmet food and meditation probably help."

"No worries. I'm glad you're going. You deserve it, and it'll be good for you."

She hugs me tight. "I love you so much," she says, putting my ice cream bowl down and sliding her hand between my legs. She leans in and puts her lips on mine. They're cold from the ice cream and I open my mouth, welcoming her tongue.

I can't remember the last time I was by myself without Wynn. I've grown more dependent on her than I care to admit. I just seem to be so hopelessly forgetful these days. Sometimes I tease her that she should never have fallen for a woman sixteen years her senior, but she brushes it off. "I love you for *who* you are, not how old or young are you," she tells me. I'll have to find a way to remind myself to take the dogs out and do all the other things I rely on her for. Still, a few days isn't that long. Surely even I can go for four days without screwing anything up?

CHAPTER SEVEN

Barker, April 2

Of all the social work students I've supervised over the years, I like Parminder Chatterjee the least. Asian students have always been my favorites because they're confident, personable, interesting and hardworking. Parminder is all of those things, but to the extreme. She comes across as brash and full of herself. Whenever I try to explain something to her, she jumps in before I can finish my sentence, trying to preempt everything I say as if she already knows it. I've explained to her that it's okay not to know something because she's here to learn, but still she insists on showing me how knowledgeable she thinks she is. Which of course she isn't. She's a first-year student who knows next to nothing about how to practice social work. I also dislike the fact that she is never on time for our supervision, a fact that irks me because my time is so limited.

While I wait for Parminder to arrive our weekly meeting, I scan my email. Job fairs, community wellness programs, library events, all information I can tell my clients about. There's a retirement party for one of the managers, a baby shower for our program assistant's daughter, and a bake sale next week to raise funds for school supplies for our clients. That's two evenings I'll be home late, and one I'll be busy baking. Parminder's favorite word is "boundaries," and she thinks doing extra-curricular events shouldn't be part of the job. I've tried to explain to her that social work is a way of life, not just a nine-to-five job, but she doesn't yet get it.

"Why would I do something outside of work hours if I don't have to? I like having my weekends to myself—I'm all about self-care." That's what she said last week, when I asked if she'd like to come to the Fun Run to raise awareness about substance abuse on Sunday afternoon. She doesn't seem to understand that we need to show our clients we're not separate from them, and that supporting their goals doesn't happen only during office hours. She tries to tell me that the new generation of social workers don't believe they have to work themselves to the bone. I don't know if she's going to cut it as a social worker.

The door opens and Parminder saunters in.

"Good afternoon Ms. Barker," she says, with no hint of apology for being fifteen minutes late. I've told her to drop the Ms., but it makes no difference.

"What's on our agenda today?" I ask her. I make it a point for all my supervisees to come with a list of topics they want to discuss. I've heard too many stories from students whose supervision sessions turned into general chat sessions with no real teaching accomplished.

She pulls out her iPhone, another thing she knows I dislike. Today's students do everything on their phones, so I have to have long discussions with them about what they're writing down, to make sure no confidentiality is breached. I still think taking notes would be easier, but it's as if these folks never even picked up a pen before.

"I'd like to discuss the family I met with last week. I made a recording of our session—with their consent of course—and I'm hoping we can listen to that."

"Good. But please don't tell me you recorded it on that phone," I say warily, since there's no sign of a tape recorder.

She smiles smugly. "Of course not," and pulls out a microscopically small device from her pocket. "Here it is."

We sit together and I listen to her session. I had asked her to meet with a couple who had just lost their foster children after the maternal grandmother won a battle for guardianship. The four children were delightful and I knew it must be quite a loss for the foster parents.

She starts out by asking them how they feel.

"We're okay," says the father.

"I see you have tears in your eyes, Mrs. Korajec. This is hard for you isn't it?" Parminder says.

I stop the tape.

"That was a really nice observation, Parminder," I tell her. "You did a lot with just that one sentence. You acknowledged that Mr. Korajec and his wife might not be feeling exactly the same way, you told Mrs. Korajec that you are paying close attention to what's going on, you gave her an opening to talk about her feelings, and you normalized what she undoubtedly was feeling at that time." Even though I don't like my student, I still like to give praise where praise is due.

"Yes, I thought it was pretty good, too," she says, and I find myself wishing that just for once she could show a little humility. "And as you'll hear, Mrs. Korajec burst into tears after I said that, and told me just how hard it's been. Which led to Mr. Korajec telling her she's too sensitive and if she can't deal with separating from the kids, perhaps she better not be a foster parent."

We listen to more of the tape.

"Did any of this remind you of other losses you've had?" Parminder asks Mrs. Korajec. "I believe both your parents are deceased."

I stop the tape.

"This is where we have to draw a fine line. You're a caseworker, not a clinician or therapist. So you have to be careful not to enter into what might become a therapy session. Your first intervention of acknowledging Mrs. Korajec's feelings was a good one, but this one is a little too personal. You're a caseworker and this is opening up a can of worms you want to keep closed. If you think Mrs. Korajec is too wrapped up in grief, then by all means you can suggest to her that she see a therapist, but we are basically here to focus on the children."

"I understand, but I disagree. I think Mrs. Korajec appreciated my intervention."

"I'm not denying that, but you have to understand your role. You're a first-year social work student, not a trained psychologist." She looks miffed that I'm criticizing her. "Now let's talk about you." I pull my chair a little closer to hers. "How do you feel about the kids being transferred?"

"I think it's terrible. It completely lets the birth mom off the hook. Now that the kids are with Granny, Mom won't bother to work her family reunification plan. Mom's visitation is meant to be supervised, but if the kids are with Granny, they'll just be acting like one big, happy family. And who knows how long that will even last? There's a reason Mom turned out the way she did. Who knows if Granny's any better?"

"You don't have much sympathy for birth parents do you?"

"No. Why have kids in the first place if you're not going to love and cherish them? I hate that these people do it so haphazardly without any thought of whether they can afford the kids, or even whether they want them. It reminds me of where my grandparents live in India. So many unwanted children, so many orphanages, so little access to birth control. But here women have access to birth control, so they have no excuse not to use it."

It's the longest speech I've heard Parminder make since we started working together and definitely the most honest. I'm glad that she's starting to trust me enough that she'll voice negative opinions, but I'm concerned that her opinions aren't those of our profession. In my first day of social work school one of the students put her hand up and asked, "Is it true we have to be a bleeding-heart liberal to do this job?" We all laughed, but secretly we'd all had the same thought.

"Sounds like you'd like to take all the kids from lousy birth parents and not give them a second chance."

"I think the system is way too easy on them, yes."

"I wonder if you'd feel differently if you'd actually had the task of separating children from their parents? When I was in my first job after school, I had to remove the cutest, most darling little three-year-old from her mom, knowing she would never see her again because mom had used up all her last chances. I can still hear the sobs and screams as I left with the little girl. It was heart wrenching, and I suspect neither mom nor daughter ever forgot that moment. Birth moms love their kids, even when they don't know how to parent them."

"But she must have done something wrong if you took the child away."

"Yes, she did, but that's not the point."

"By all means, give me the chance to remove a child from an abusive home, I'll jump at it."

"What about when you have to remove a child from a good home, like the Korajecs? How will you manage that?"

"I'll be fine. I would never let my feelings get in the way of my job," she says with such supreme confidence that I have to wonder whether she actually has any feelings.

"It's important to know whether or not you can work in the welfare system." I tell her. "It's not for everybody. We all have to find our own niche. Luckily, the world of social work is a big one. Speaking of which, have you thought about where you'll do next year's placement?"

"One of my classmates suggested I work at the county psychiatric hospital. She thought I might really enjoy it."

"Interesting. Your classmate is right that some people find it fascinating. I think for those of us who tend toward judging people a little, it's a good place to be, because we all know that people with severe mental illness have absolutely no power or control over the lot they were given in life." As I say this, I have to wonder whether Parminder could, in fact, find some reason to judge the person who shuffles up and down the hospital corridor all day long, cowering when a doctor tries to approach, convinced that the nurses are FBI agents.

"What about this summer? Some of my past students have done an international volunteer placement. There are some amazing internships all over the world—Africa, Asia, South America."

"I guess I'll have to tag along with my family to visit my grandparents in Mumbai."

"Not if you tell them that doing a volunteer placement will improve your standing at school."

She cocks her head to one side. "You have a point," she admits. "And it would be a good way to improve my Spanish. Might make me even more marketable than I already am." My eyes widen at her arrogance and she adds quickly, "you know, because I'm a minority student," she adds. I groan inwardly.

"Would you like me to bring you some information to next week's supervision?" I start to gather up my stuff, signaling that we're almost done.

"Sure," she says and I wonder whether she really wants it, or whether she's just humoring me. It sounds as if she might like an excuse not to drag along with her family to the Indian subcontinent this summer. Maybe doing a social work volunteer project in a different part of the world will also give her a little more empathy to those who are less fortunate.

As for me, I'm looking forward to the end of her school year and hoping that next year's intern is a little more humble. Meanwhile, a plan is coming to mind with a task that will really test her mettle.

CHAPTER EIGHT

Barker, April 9

I need to broach Wynn on a very delicate subject and I'm trying to decide how best to do it. She's been getting very forgetful. I realize that after a certain age, which thankfully I haven't reached yet, everyone has senior moments, and I know she'd be the first to admit she's flaky, but I have to get her to see that it's more than that. I can't figure out how to do it, and then, as luck would have it, an opportunity falls right into my lap.

"I'd really like to see that new movie with Julianne Moore. It just opened at the Regal," Wynn tells me when I get home from work.

"The one about the woman who gets Alzheimer's?" I ask.

"Yes, it sounds interesting."

It's been a long, exhausting day. All my home visits were difficult. Mr. Phillips was complaining that the kids only talk to Mrs. Phillips and ignore his presence altogether. I tried to reassure him and explain that it's not unusual for kids who grew up in single-parent homes, or had abusive fathers. I didn't tell him that even when that's not the case, foster kids seem to have a gift for triangulating foster parents so that Mom thinks they're wonderful and Dad resents them, or vice versa. People call those kids manipulative but I've never thought they do it on purpose. Then I spent an hour trying to persuade Mrs. Lopez to keep a five-year-old who yelled solidly for four hours without letting up. I reminded her about the part in the foster parent training where she had to imagine herself being ripped from her own home and placed with strangers in a strange city.

At my next visit, I had to placate two siblings who hate the home I placed them in. I can't blame them; even though Mom has all the qualifications, she's a cold fish, very standoffish, and they're used to being in a noisy, rambunctious environment. It took me so long to finish my visits that I haven't even started on any of my paperwork. But Wynn's suggestion that we go see a movie about a middle-aged woman who gets dementia, is too good an opportunity to miss.

"What time does it start?" I ask, and am rewarded by her look of surprised pleasure that I'm up for going out on a weeknight, instead of collapsing in front of the TV. I've already read the book, but Wynn hasn't. I thought of her when I was reading it. I'm interested to see what reactions she has to it.

***

After the movie, Wynn asks if I want to go to our favorite ice cream parlor and even though I'm almost passed out with exhaustion at this point, I say yes.

"What did you think?" I ask her as we sit down, her with a hot fudge sundae and me with a peach melba. I'm hoping the sugar kicks some life into me.

"It was good, though I'm not sure if I could say I liked it. The part where she's introduced to her son's girlfriend, and then a few moments later she introduces herself as if they've never met, that was scary."

"Scary?"

"Yes, because in other ways she was still so normal. There she was, making this complicated meal, which she did perfectly, and then doing something really whacky."

"Reminded me of you," I venture, chuckling as if it's a joke.

"Tell me about it! I could see myself doing the same thing—being so focused on making the perfect dish that I would screen out anything else from my consciousness," she says, spooning ice cream absentmindedly into her mouth.

"So if you did what she did, it wouldn't be about not

remembering, it would be about not focusing?"

"I think so. There's a difference between forgetting something and never putting it into your memory in the first place. You should know, how often do you berate me for not paying attention to things?" she says with a sigh. I roll my eyes; it's an ongoing issue between us. How many times have I asked her impatiently, "How could you not notice that?" Once, when she was staying over with her mom for a couple of nights, I decided to surprise her by repainting our bathroom. When she got back, I waited and waited for her to mention it. In and out she went, unpacking her toiletries, peeing, and eventually I asked her what she thought of the new color. She looked startled, headed back to the bathroom, and came out looking sheepish. I mean, really, how could anyone not notice that?

"It was interesting to see the way the movie showed how long it took her family to realize what was going on. It was because she was still very functional on lots of levels," Wynn continues.

"Right. Outsiders spotted it quicker than they did, because her family was used to her being ditzy," I respond. "But honey, you know, it did make me think." She looks at me and her eyebrows furrow into a question.

"About me?" she says and I take the plunge.

"Well, yes, about you and about us. I'm so used to you being flaky, that it takes me a while to notice any substantive change. But lately… I have to admit, I've noticed a few things. I don't think they're just about you not paying attention. I think your memory's really starting to play tricks on you."

She goes quiet and I wonder if I've gone too far. She scrapes the bottom of the glass with her spoon, trying to get every last drop of chocolate syrup.

"I've noticed that too," she says quietly.

I cut a chunk of peach and mix it with a spoonful of vanilla ice cream before putting it in my mouth. I let her words hang in the air, so that we both know she said them.

"How about if you make an appointment to see a psychiatrist?" I want to bring up this suggestion in a soft and gentle way, but I can't think of any way to sugarcoat it. "Or a neurologist?"

"Really? You think I should?"

"It might put your mind at ease. Both of our minds. It's

probably nothing. But if they did think something was going on, you could get on medication while it's still helpful."

"You know what?" she looks suddenly animated as she wipes a bit of chocolate off her lower lip, and I think she's going to agree, but her words dispel any such idea. "It didn't help her much in the movie did it? That doctor figured out what was going on, put her on medication, and she still deteriorated. I think if that's what's in store for me, I'd rather just go downhill quickly, not prolong the agony."

"Honey, everyone's different. She was really young, that's why it progressed so quickly. But you hear of lots of people who take Aricept or Namenda and it changes their lives."

"All of a sudden you're an expert on dementia?"

I'm surprised by her harsh tone. An article I read recently noted that people with memory problems often become belligerent but this is a little shocking. I feel tears well up in the corners of my eyelids and brush them away quickly. She looks up from her empty glass and sees me dabbing my eyes.

"Sweetie, I'm sorry. I didn't mean to get defensive. This is just a hard conversation to have. If you think I should see a psychiatrist, then I will, okay?"

I smile and feel a weight lifted off my shoulders.

"I can help you make calls if you want," I offer and she shrugs.

***

On the way home I think about the siblings I visited today. Summer will be here soon, and I always feel bad for the kids who don't get real vacations. As a social worker, you can make suggestions to the parents but if they don't take you up on them, there's not much you can do about it. Last year Juanita, one of my single moms who worked full time, was too scared to let the twelve-year-old girl she was fostering go out on the street to play with other kids, so she just kept her at home all day. I told Juanita about summer camps but she couldn't afford them. She told Sarita it was a staycation and stocked the house with ice cream and sodas and told her she could use the computer as much and as often as she wanted. The girl taught herself coding and became a real computer nerd by the end of summer. But I felt bad that when her teacher asked Sarita what she did with her summer, apparently the only thing she could come up with was how many dungeons she'd opened on *A Link Between Worlds*.

"Did I tell you about the summer sponsorship program Celia and I are setting up at work?" I ask Wynn as we sit at a prolonged traffic light.

"I don't think so…but now I'm going to worry every time you start a question with, 'did I tell you?'"

I laugh. "Then I won't do that anymore. I'm pretty sure I didn't tell you. Celia and I were talking about our summers when we were kids and how different it is for the fosters. Her parents were scientists so she did all these enrichment programs, which were super cool, even if they did make her realize she never wanted to be a scientist. I attended a really fun camp, where we did everything: water sports, horseback riding, arts and crafts, treasure hunts, writing, and producing plays. It opened my eyes to a world beyond Dad's lawyering and Mom's teaching. Celia and I thought it would be really great if our kids could do stuff like that, but most of my foster parents need every penny of the foster care stipend just to make ends meet, so they don't have any money to spare."

"I thought the city ran day camps?"

"They do. But that's just glorified babysitting. I'm talking about enrichment, where kids get to learn about space exploration, or marine biology or things that could really change their lives. So Celia and I decided to set up a scholarship fund the public can donate to, so our kids can do some cool stuff over the summer."

"That's great! I mean, I can't believe you're taking on something else, in addition to everything you already do, but the kids will love it." I smile. Wynn's always supportive of everything I do. "Can we make a donation?" she asks.

I had a feeling that once I told her about the scholarship, she'd offer to give money to the program. Wynn is generous to a fault. "I wish we could, but it would be a boundary violation for me to do it." I pause. "Although I suppose since we're not married, if it came from your separate business account, that might be okay. You could probably even claim it on taxes."

"Oh that's not important." Wynn checks the mirror then pulls across the street into our driveway.

"I'll look into it, and let you know, okay?" I tell her and then before we get out of the car, we both turn to each other and get ourselves into an enormous bear hug.

"I love you," we whisper simultaneously, and I think, this evening couldn't have gone any better.

CHAPTER NINE

Wynn, April 15

Dr. Larson's house is a Spanish Colonial, set back from the street. I can see the terracotta roof tiles and the white adobe even before we pull into the driveway. This style of home always makes me feel as if I'm in Mexico. As I pass the ornate wrought-iron gate, I see a plaque on it, but since I'm driving, I don't have time to read it.

"I didn't notice," Barker says. "Perhaps her home is on the historical register, or perhaps it had her professional information on it."

"Why would it have that?" I ask as I drive down the gorgeous driveway.

"Her private practice is in her home. I told you that."

As we step out of the car, we walk through a patio with a marble fountain in the middle. To the right is a graceful archway that leads to a large wooden door with black iron hinges, which I presume is the front door. I'm about to head toward it but Barker steers me to the left where curved steps, inlaid with those hand-painted Mexican tiles we love, lead up to a balcony.

"She told me to use the entrance with the steps," she explains as we start climbing.

We've never been invited here before but Barker says if she's to get a supervisor position, she needs to have allies at work. The other day we had one of the mental health supervisors over for dinner. She was nice enough, although I felt like everything I said was being analyzed and diagnosed. But Barker seems determined to get that supervisor position, as evidenced by yet another social event with a colleague. She told me that Dr. Larson is the best psychologist in the agency. I asked her who else is invited and she looked at me a little oddly and said, "it's just us. You said you wanted me to come with you," which is weird, since I think I'm the one accompanying her.

"Just be your usual self," she said.

We climb the steps to the little balcony and I'm surprised to see that the door leading into the house is open. There's even a sign that says, "This way, please." Perhaps Dr. Larson is as eccentric as I am. We walk through the entryway and right away, a woman comes forward to greet us. I notice her jewelry right away—big, clunky, and chic—and her hair, which is dyed jet-black. I gave up dying my hair years ago. I'd like to say it's salt and pepper but actually it's more like dried-up oatmeal.

"Right on time!" says the woman who I presume is Dr. Larson. I'm surprised that it should matter for a social invitation but perhaps Barker has already told her about my propensity to be late. She ushers us into a small, living room where she has a comfortable-looking sofa, a couple of upright leather armchairs and a desk in the corner.

"Would you like some water?" she asks. I'm a little surprised she doesn't offer a choice of drink, but then again, it's a hot day so I figure water makes sense. We both nod affirmatively.

We sit on the sofa together and Dr. Larson sits in one of the upright chairs.

"So, you're Wynn," she says.

"Nice to meet you," I respond. "I've heard a lot about you."

"I'm so glad you could come today. I know you might have some misgivings." I wonder why. She must be referring to office politics.

"No worries," I say, hoping we're not going to spend all our time talking about how to finagle Barker's promotion. "Whatever Barker wants, Barker gets," I sing to the tune of "Whatever Lola Wants," and Dr. Larson looks a little shocked. I wonder whether I should tone myself down, but Barker's such a serious person and doubtless this doctor is too, so I think it might be a good idea if I can help them both lighten up.

"So," Dr. Larson says, turning specifically to me, "let's get started. Do you know what I do?" This strikes me as exceedingly odd way to start a conversation, but I decide to take her at face value.

"Yes. You're a psychologist. You work at Barker's agency. She thinks you're pretty cool, actually. That's why we're here."

Dr. Larson smiles. "Psychiatrist actually, and I'm not sure that's the exact reason, but I'm glad she trusts me, and I hope you do too."

I sneak a glance at Barker to see if she finds this conversation as peculiar as I do. But her gaze is on the bookshelves, where large tomes nestle next to each other. I left my glasses in the car, so I can't make out their titles from here, but if I had to hazard a guess, I would say that they're professional books rather than Danielle Steele novels.

"Tell me how you and Barker got together," she says. I like people who are direct, and I like when they want to know how we met.

"Why don't you tell her, Barker?" I don't want to monopolize the conversation and Barker has barely said a word. But she shakes her head.

"No, you go ahead, honey."

"It's one of those typical lesbian love stories," I say. "She was dating a woman called Jan and I was dating Linda. Jan and Linda were best friends so we used to go out as a foursome. Well, then Jan started seeing another woman called Bev, and unbeknownst to me, Linda started having an affair with Bev's girlfriend—"

"Whoa!" Dr. Larson cuts me off. "This is getting way too complicated. I don't know how you can even remember all this!"

"Okay, you got me. It's not really how we met, it's just how every other lesbian couple we know got together. Barker and I met at a fundraiser but that's a much less interesting story. I'd never be able to remember a story that complicated. I have a terrible memory." I smile ruefully and take a sip of water from the bottle she gave me. I remember the days when hostesses provided water in glasses, with ice, and then offered fruit or cookies to their guests, but nowadays shoving a plastic bottle into someone's hand seems to be about it.

"Tell me more about your memory problems," Dr. Larson says and I think, boy once a doctor, always a doctor. Can't she just talk about the Rays or the Buccaneers? But still, I humor her.

"My mom had dementia, so naturally I worry that I'll get it too. It's hard to know what's menopausal fog, what's a senior moment, and what could be a real sign of something more serious. In fact, Barker keeps telling me I should get evaluated, but I really don't think it's that bad yet."

Dr. Larson glances over at Barker, who smiles in an absent kind of way. "Since you mention your memory, let's do a little exam. I'm going to tell you three things to remember and I'll ask you what they are in a few minutes, okay?"

"You want to see if I'm gaga yet?" I laugh. "Fine by me." This woman definitely has odd social graces, but if I can get a free memory test, why not?

She tells me the three words. "Shirt. Brown. Honesty," and looks up at me. I wonder if she's waiting for me to repeat them, but I decide I'd rather steer the conversation in a different direction.

"This place is gorgeous. How long have you owned it?" I ask. She looks a little taken aback, like she's the one meant to be asking questions. But she can't help herself from answering because who doesn't like to talk about their home?

"A few years now. It was a fixer-upper. I made the plans and bought all the materials, and then had some day laborers do the work."

"It turned out beautifully. Those tiles in the staircase look Mexican. Did you bring them back yourself?"

"Hardly." She laughs, though not with her full belly, just a polite little chuckle. "They'd be awfully heavy. There's a store in town that has everything Mexican: *equipales*—you know the wicker and pigskin furniture—Talavera tiles, the *marmol* fountain you saw out front."

"Well, it's beautiful," I turn to Barker. "Isn't it, sweetie?"

"Yes, delightful," she responds and then falls quiet again. It's not like her to be so silent and I wonder what's going on with her.

"Back to those three words, I gave you," says Dr. Larson. "What were they?"

I'm startled. I totally forgot about them. I meant to repeat them to myself, but to be honest, I wasn't even paying that much attention when she said them.

"No idea," I answer, smiling.

"Let me give you some prompts," she says, but I'm tired of this. I'd rather talk more about her house.

"Nah, that's okay. I'm fine with not knowing them, trust me. There's too much in life to remember without having to put things into my brain that I'll never need again. Tell me where that store is in town. I'd love to get some of those black iron sconces for our patio."

She gives us the address then says, "Let's try something different. I'm going to give you some words and you're going to tell me what makes them alike. If I were to ask you how an arm and a leg are similar, how would you respond?"

I really think this woman is weird, but I'm here for Barker so I answer. "How about: if I were to see you professionally, you'd probably charge me an arm and a leg?"

Dr. Larson sighs and turns to Barker. "I think this is probably enough. How about we talk more tomorrow at work?"

I get that Barker needs allies at work, but I'm not sure if I would trust this woman. She may be an excellent professional at work but she sure as heck is a weird human being. I'm kinda glad when she stands up, intimating that our visit is over. I shake her hand politely and we make our way back down the curved staircase. This is one colleague of Barker's I won't be in a hurry to see again. The things we do for love, I think. And then I start humming that song with the same title.

CHAPTER TEN

Barker, April 16

"How bad is it?"

I'm at work and have finally caught enough of a break that I can go chat with Dr. Larson, or Elizabeth, as she's asked me to call her. I knock on her door and she invites me in. She has one of the nicer offices in our suite. In one corner, there's a rack of dress-up clothes; archetypal princesses and monsters used by children who can't verbalize their feelings but can act them out. In another corner is a sand-tray, and behind it a shelf with glove puppets and stuffed animals. Elizabeth is sitting at her desk, typing into her computer.

"Come in, come in." She smiles warmly and waves me to a seat opposite her as she continues to tap rapidly at her keyboard. "In the old days, I'd have had such a high pile of files sitting on this desk everyone would know how behind I am on the documentation and leave me alone. But with electronic medical records, my desk is so clean for all anyone knows I'm totally on top of things and just sitting here playing solitaire!"

"I'm sorry. I can come back—"

"No, no, I didn't mean to imply that. I always have time for you." She looks up and locks her eyes on mine, and I feel a little flutter in my stomach. Is she flirting with me?

"I know what you mean," I respond. "We used to be able to diagnose people based on the state of their desk—messy piles of external chaos everywhere versus obsessive-compulsive neatness—and now we can't do that."

She smiles. "I might have judged them for it, the way I judge myself, but hopefully I never made that spontaneous a diagnosis." She pushes her chair away from the desk.

"Talking of diagnosing people, how bad is it, with Wynn?"

She looks at me with an expression of sympathy in her eyes. "Hold on. I didn't want to put anything on the computer, so let me retrieve my notes." She fishes into a tan leather briefcase at her side. "Even without notes I can tell you she definitely comes across as confused. I think your suspicions of dementia are probably pretty accurate."

Before she agreed to see Wynn, I had told Elizabeth some of what I'd noticed with Wynn over the last few months.

"So that's what you think she has?"

"It certainly seems that way, although obviously that wasn't a full evaluation." I nod my head. I'm not surprised that she's corroborating my layperson's diagnosis.

"Can you tell me specifically what you saw that leads you to that conclusion?" I ask her, ready to take my own notes.

"A number of things. I presume you told her exactly who she was coming to see and why?"

"Absolutely. I mentioned that you recently started at our agency because you wanted some experience with children, but that before that you worked extensively with older adults and that you're considered one of the best neuro-psychiatrists in the county. We'd discussed the possibility of her seeing a psychiatrist or a neurologist and although she was hesitant, in the end she agreed that it would be a good thing. But as I told you before you agreed to meet with her, getting an appointment through the regular channels would have taken months. I called a bunch of people on the list our insurance company gave me, and the soonest appointment was four months away. So when you said we could come to your private practice office, I was thrilled. And she certainly wasn't against coming, though she did mumble something about everything always being about my workplace."

"I wondered about that. It was almost as if she thought you were paying a social visit. She didn't seem to realize this was an appointment at all. But given that it was, I saw an odd mix of deteriorating cognitive skills along with a real sharpness and a sense that she's still pretty on top of certain things. Which isn't unusual for people with dementia, especially in the early stages. Often the dementia's only apparent in one sphere of life, and they're still extremely functional in other areas."

This matches my own research. I've been reading a lot about dementia, and there have been a spate of documentaries that all show how someone can be very functional in some areas and completely out of it in others. Wynn fits right in.

"As you probably realized, I was attempting to do a mental status examination with the questions I asked. She completely failed the memory part—people usually make a real effort to try to remember the three words. When they can't, they'll often make an excuse like saying that they weren't important enough to remember, which is what Wynn did. It's the same thing with orientation to time. Often when I ask people what day or month it is, they tell me that those kinds of things aren't important to them anymore so they don't hold on to them. That's the tricky thing with dementia; people can still come across as highly functional, and it's only their immediate family who notice the little things that don't sit right."

A lot of what she's saying isn't new. I did notice how Wynn made the comment about not wanting to hold onto the words because they weren't important enough, and I thought, if it were me, I'd want to prove to the doctor that I could do it, I'd want to impress her so that she could reassure me that I was fine.

"I also observed that she used humor to cover up what she didn't know, which is also common among my clients. When I asked her what was similar about an arm and a leg, she made a joke. I can't tell you how many times people have made jokes like that when they can't come up with the correct answer." She leans toward me, her arms reaching forward on the table, hands clasped together. "I need to ask you something. I'm talking to you somewhat as professional to professional. But we're talking about your partner, not a colleague. How are you doing with all this?" She's sitting at her desk, and I'm sitting in the patient chair and as she leans forward, I feel as if I'm in therapy.

"It's not anything I wasn't prepared for," I answer.

"That's not what I asked. I asked how you're feeling," she says, getting up and walking over to my side of her desk. Her empathy is touching and I feel moisture forming in the corners of my eyes. "It's hard stuff, Barker. Very hard." She sits next to me and I'm struck by the soft scent of patchouli and the warmth in her milky-grey eyes. A wave of hair falls across her brow and I wish I could lean over and push it back. In some ways she reminds me of Wynn when I first met her: long limbs, tight body, and an undefined feeling of sensuality that exudes from her, even as she's telling me my partner may have a very serious illness.

"It's not just her memory I'm concerned about. I've read that people with dementia can also come across as paranoid, and can start doing things that are completely out of character. Should I be worried about that?"

"Certainly. Many people think Alzheimer's is just a case of memory loss. But in many ways, the brain is being taken over—at this point, we think by beta-amyloids—and so it starts to give commands that it wouldn't normally give. People who've been sweet and charming all their lives suddenly become suspicious of those around them. If they lose something, they think you stole it. If they don't understand what you're saying, they think you're out to get them. And because their mind is playing tricks on them, they can start to do things that are completely out of character. But hopefully that would be a long way down the road, and it might not even happen at all. The first thing you should do is get Wynn to agree to a full workup with a specialist who can monitor her. That's not something I can do in my private practice. But what I could do is write her a prescription for Aricept or Namenda."

"Is it a cure?"

"No, but it might help slow down whatever's going on with her."

"I'm not sure she'd be willing to take it. What would I tell her?"

"Some of my patients' families tell them it's a multivitamin, or some other benign kind of pill, but I don't think that's what you want to do with Wynn. She did mention that she's got a hopeless memory, so why not just tell her it will help her remember things?"

"She's not big on taking drugs of any kind."

"What does she have to lose? There aren't any terrible side effects from it. Some people have mentioned headaches and nightmares, but it won't do any harm to her. Why not suggest she give it a three-month trial and see how she feels after that?" Elizabeth pulls out her prescription pad.

"Sure," I say. "Why not? Like you say, it can't do any harm."

After she writes it up, she puts her arm around me and her eyes are filled with sympathy.

"This might be a long road you're going to travel, Barker. Any time you want to talk, my office door is always open to you."

I feel my heart expand. Everyone needs to have someone who will be totally on their side, who will be there when needed. Lately, Wynn hasn't felt completely like that person any more. Knowing there's someone else who can be a support feels great.

Now I just have to get Wynn to take the medication.

CHAPTER ELEVEN

Wynn, May 1

There are five women in my class and I ask them to introduce themselves and tell us why they chose this course.

The first to speak is an almost bald-headed, middle aged African American woman dressed in baggy sweats.

"Hi. I'm Connie. I love doing crafts. I've crocheted blankets and knitted sweaters, but I've never made jewelry before. I want to do something new to take my mind off the chemo." She rubs her head and everyone smiles in sympathy.

Next is a young woman with jet-black hair and a pierced nostril. She reminds me of the recent spate of movies about tough-looking straight girls with tattoos.

"Hi, I'm Zerella?" she says as if it's a question, and I'm caught off-guard by the dissonance of her image with her voice, which is like an eleven-year-old Valley girl. "I've never made anything before, but my therapist suggested I take this class to help me get over my social anxiety."

I'm surprised by what I've heard from these two women. It didn't occur to me that people would have ulterior motives for coming to my class. I'd imagined that everyone was there because they'd always wanted to learn how to make wire-wrapped jewelry. I can't help smiling at the candidness of their disclosures. My mom was from England and she could never get over how Americans love to share intimate details with strangers. She came from an era when illnesses all had euphemisms, you didn't even say the "C" word aloud, and you would never tell anyone you saw a therapist, let alone the reason why.

The third woman to talk is dressed in a white shirt and white shorts and looks more likely to be on a tennis court than in a jewelry-making class.

"Hi I'm Ava. I heard about this class, and it sounded like fun."

Good. I'm glad there's someone who isn't using me as an art therapist, because I never signed up to be one.

The other two women, Rosalie and Cheryl, are friends who came to the class together and who have been making jewelry for years. They sound like they may know more than I do, and I'm not quite sure why they signed up, other than that the class was a convenient day and time for them.

"Okay, let's get started. I want you to cut six nine-inch pieces of 20-gauge wire. That's this wire that's right in front of you." The women lunge forward to grab the wire, as if it may run out. I have three sets of nose pliers and it looks like Rosalie and Cheryl also have a pair so we're good to go. The women pick up their tools and after they've cut their wire into pieces, I show them how to wrap each piece into a spiral.

"Now, make another spiral from the other end to the center, making sure the spirals face in opposite directions so you have an 'S' shape." Rosalie and Cheryl do so and then take the other pieces of wire and do the same. They have clearly done this before. I start to wonder whether they were sent to check on me, to see if I know what I'm doing. Connie and Ava watch them and follow their lead.

Zerella fusses with the pliers and I see that her hands are shaking.

"Are you okay?" I ask her.

"I don't think I can do this," she whispers, putting down the pliers.

"How about if you just sit and watch us for today and then maybe next week you'll feel more comfortable?"

"Could I do that?"

"Sure, why not? You've paid for the class and the materials."

We settle into a rhythm, folding the "S" shapes and pulling

out the centers so we create little cages for the beads. I show them how to insert beads into the cages and then how to connect the spirals.

As we work, Ava turns to Connie.

"I don't mean to intrude, but can I ask what type of cancer?"

"Carcinoma Meningitis. It's basically a type of brain cancer. I had breast cancer a few years ago and it put me at heightened risk for this type. I'm doing pretty well though, I think."

"I've never heard of it. But I certainly know all about meningitis. My twin daughters both contracted it when they were in college."

"Are they okay now?"

"No." Ava pauses. "No, actually they both died within forty-eight hours."

The whole table stops working. Connie looks startled and Zerella starts shaking again. "Oh my god, that's terrible," Rosalie and Cheryl say together.

"I'm sorry." Ava looks contrite. "I didn't mean to upset anyone. I don't really talk about it that often. I don't know why I brought it up."

"You don't have to apologize," says Connie. "I think we were all a little shocked. But it's your story and if you're comfortable talking about it, the least we can do is bear witness."

There's a lull for a moment and the women start dipping into the box of beads to decide which ones they want to use in their jewelry. I figure it's my turn to step in and steer us onto safer subjects.

"Let me show you how to make hook clasps and figure eight links so you can attach the beads to each other," I say, picking up my pliers and demonstrating how to create the connectors. Everyone looks grateful and focuses in on completing their earrings. Before I know it, our time is up.

"Will I see you all next week?" I ask, wondering whether either the crafting or the conversation has put anyone off. Connie says she has a conflict for the following week, and I wonder whether it's chemo. Zerella says she'll talk to her mom and decide whether she's going to return. I tell the other three I'm looking forward to our next class and shoo them out the door so that I can clean up.

All in all, I think that although today's class wasn't quite what I was expecting, it went pretty well.

***

As I head to the parking lot, I see that Ava is waiting by the exit.

"Can we talk for a few minutes, maybe grab a cup of coffee?"

I'm about to decline, thinking that I have to get home to make dinner for Barker, but then I remember she told me she'd be working late this evening.

"Sure," I say, and we walk across the street to a pleasant-looking coffee shop.

"Do you think I was too much for them?" she asks after we're seated with cups of iced lattes.

"I don't know. People aren't used to hearing about such devastating events in what they think is going to be a casual conversation."

"I know. I don't know why I blurted it out. I think it's because I never tell anyone about it, and somehow this seemed like a safe place." She stirs her latte and I can see she's trying really hard not to cry.

"That's what being with a group of women will do for you. Gives us an automatic sense of comfort." I take a sip of latte and realize I forgot to put sweetener in. I pick up a packet of Equal and shake some into my drink. "What do you do when you're not taking fun classes?" I ask to lighten up the mood and also because I'm not sure I want to hear too much more about dead children.

"I'm a foster parent. That takes up quite a bit of my time."

"Isn't that hard? Especially after losing your daughters. Do you have other kids?"

"No. After the girls died, I was too old to start a new family. But I'd been a parent for so long, I didn't know what else to do. And this keeps me distracted."

"What are they like? The kids you have now." I try to imagine the difference between parenting your own daughters and taking in someone else's kids, children who probably wish they could just be home with their original families.

"They're typical teenagers, into hair, makeup, fashion."

"Are they pretty?"

Ava looks a little taken aback. "Why do you ask?"

"I just thought having two teenage girls who are attractive could be a bit of a worry. You never know what kind of trouble they might get into."

"Well that's true for any children. Do you have kids?"

"No. Never wanted them to be honest."

"I think it's one of those things. Either you do, or you don't. I don't judge anyone who doesn't have them, or doesn't want them."

"What about the parents of the kids you foster. Do you judge them?" I think about some of the grisly stories I've heard from Barker.

"Most of them never had a chance in life. They had lousy parenting, or got caught up with the wrong guy. They're poor, uneducated—and we don't make it easy for them."

"We?"

"Society. As soon as they're caught up in the system, they get judged for things regular parents can get away with because they don't have social workers hovering over them all the time."

"Some of my best friends are social workers." I feel myself getting defensive. I could mention Barker but for all I know she might know this woman. "Anyway, what's the alternative?"

"Well, I've sometimes thought that it would make more sense if the county gave the money they pay me to look after those kids, directly to birth mothers. If they had that money, they probably wouldn't get into the trouble they do."

"I don't know about that." I think about the people who use whatever money they have to buy drugs and alcohol. "It's not a lack of money for some of those folks. I think they choose their drugs or their boyfriends over their kids. That's what my birth mom did." I surprise myself telling her this. I never tell anyone about this part of my background. Even Barker doesn't know.

"Yes, but it's not really a choice is it? If they don't have income, they have to stay with the abusive father."

"Nobody makes them do drugs. Sometimes I think the fact that they know there's some nice middle-class woman like you waiting in the wings to provide a home for their kids lets them off the hook. They don't seem to realize that even if the kids are in a good home, the fact that they've been abandoned makes them more likely to end up like their moms. Sometimes I wish I could just shake them and say, 'look at what you're doing to your kids. You're ruining their lives as well as your own.'"

"I think a lot of them know that. They feel hopeless and helpless."

"You sound just like—" I'm about to say Barker again. It's hard to have a conversation about foster care without mentioning her. "You sound just like all my social worker friends," I improvise quickly.

"I guess that's why I make a good foster mother," Ava says, and drains the last of her latte from her glass. She looks at her watch. "Speaking of which, I need to pick up my girls from school. Thanks for the class, and for the chat. Maybe we can do this again."

"I'd like that," I say. It's been a long time since I made a new friend. Barker always tells me she would be crossing a professional boundary to make friends with her students, but I don't think it's the same for a community center teacher.

After she leaves, I pick up the newspaper that's been abandoned on the chair next to mine. And that's when I see that today isn't the day Barker's working late. Today is Wednesday, our date night, and she told me she was going to make an extra effort to come home early because we have tickets for the local theater and I was meant to be making us dinner to eat before we go.

Damn. Why can I never keep things straight anymore? I've been taking Aricept for two weeks now, but it's obviously not working.

KALLIE

CHAPTER TWELVE

June 13

After the lady who brought us here leaves, I realize my stomach is grumbling furiously. I turn to John and ask if it would be okay if I fixed us something for lunch.

"You don't have to ask," he says. "Just go right ahead."

The freezer is full of ready-made meals, but I decide I want to be really grown up and prepare something for us. I don't know how to do much because most foster homes won't let us near the kitchen. They're scared we might secret away a butcher knife, steal the food, or eat the special treats they were keeping for themselves. I look in the fridge and see ingredients for a salad.

"Why don't you two go into the living room," I say to John and Mikki, as if I'm the mom making lunch for us all. They walk toward the large window overlooking the bay and stand by it, looking out. I chop lettuce, tomato, and cucumbers and put them in a large bowl, then toss the salad with ranch dressing. I find cold cuts and make us all baloney sandwiches. There are chips in the pantry and I put a few on each plate. Then I load everything on a tray and take it into the living room.

"Shall we sit at the dining table, or on the sofas?" I ask, but Mikki and John are so deep in conversation they don't seem to even hear me. Mikki is standing very close to John and because they have their backs to me, I can see that the hand he's using to express something is about to make a landing on her butt. I clear my throat loudly. "Table or sofas?" I practically yell.

They turn around.

"Let's sit here," he says, patting the love seat. He puts himself in the middle. It's a bit of a squeeze, and his thigh is jammed up against mine, but he's so good-looking, I don't really care.

"So," he says as he picks up his sandwich. "How well do you two know each other?"

We tell him some of our stories from foster care and he laughs and groans in all the right places.

"You two sure have some stories to tell," he says, patting our knees, one hand on each side.

"Mrs. Clark's was the best place. She got us involved in tennis, which we love and we're good at." I can't seem to stop talking. I think it's because beneath the steel-rimmed glasses, he has really sexy eyes. "We even brought our rackets with us." I point to them sitting in the entryway.

"Yeah, well, I don't think you'll be playing tennis while you're here," he says. I can see the courts far below us, so I don't know why we wouldn't be able to play.

"Did you bring your swimsuits?" he asks.

I roll my eyes. "Of course! Who would come to a condo like this and not bring one?" Not that we knew we were coming here when we packed, but Mrs. Clark recently bought us new swimwear and we weren't going to leave that behind.

"Great," he says. "Why don't you go put them on."

"Aren't you going to finish your lunch?" I ask, slightly put out that he's ignoring my efforts at meal preparation. But I can't wait to get to the beach, so I don't pout too long as he shows us into our rooms.

I'm glad Mrs. Clark got us the two-pieces because up until this year, all the families I lived with said they weren't appropriate for young girls. I remember Mrs. Anderson saying, "Females who wear bikinis are just asking for it, showing men everything they've got." But Mrs. Clark was different. Two weeks ago, we were at Target with her when she asked if we had bikinis. When we told her we only had one-piece swimsuits she took us right over to the swimwear and told us we could pick anything we wanted.

"Is this too skimpy?" Mikki asked, holding up a sparkly bikini that hardly had any material at all.

Mrs. Clark shook her head. "It's so hot and you're both young and pretty, why cover yourself up?" she asked.

In my room, I wriggle into the tiny little bikini bottom and quickly put my shorts back on top of it. I'm worried you can see my crack at the back. I slip on the top, wishing I had more tit to fill it out, put my tank back over it, and return to the living room.

Mikki isn't there yet.

"What happened? You didn't put it on?" John asks me, looking at my shorts and tank.

"I figured I'd wear my clothes down to the beach."

"Who said anything about the beach? You girls are going to do some modeling. What do you think of that?"

To be honest, I don't think much of it. I'm hardly the type who wants to parade my body around. But Michaela will be thrilled. I shift my weight awkwardly from one foot to the other. John comes over and cups my face gently in his hands. He smells spicy and sweet at the same time and I feel myself starting to tingle as he runs his fingers on my cheek. I still haven't quite worked out who he is. At first, I thought he must be a social worker, but now it's pretty clear he's not. He's so good-looking it's almost frightening.

"Let's see what you have underneath those clothes," he says, stepping back. I want him to take my face in his hands again, so I slip off my shorts and tank, and then decide to strike a pose.

"You're a natural!" He picks up my cell phone and starts taking pictures. I put my hand on my hip, like they do on fashion runways, and push my almost non-existent tits up and out as far as they'll go.

"That's better!" He laughs "Now turn around." I spin around and as I do, I see Mikki standing in the doorway with an odd expression on her face. Unlike me, she didn't keep her dress on and also unlike me, she has plenty to show off in the upper department. When she sees me modeling for John, she puts her arms against her chest, trying to cover up her cleavage. John sees me looking in her direction.

"Hey, sweetheart, come on in. Your friend here was just modeling her bikini for me. Will you take a photo of both of us?"

he asks tossing her my phone. He puts his arm around my shoulder and holds me tight. After Mikki's taken the picture, he says to me, "Go ahead and put your shorts on now, if it makes you more comfortable," so I do. Then we go through the same routine of me taking a photo of the two of them with Michaela's phone.

We sit in the living room, making small talk, when suddenly John gets up. "I almost forgot. There's beer in the fridge. Let's celebrate the start of this 'vacation' in style." He puts air quotes around the word vacation and I wonder why. Perhaps he's just one of those people who put air quotes around everything. One of the kids at Mrs. Anderson's used to do that and it annoyed the heck out of me. But nothing about John annoys me. I've never hung out with anyone like him before. He's older than us, but not real old. He seems like such a man of the world, stroking his goatee while we talk, adjusting his glasses occasionally.

He brings in three bottles and I wait for him to bring in glasses but he tells us only sissies drink from glasses.

"Let's see who can down theirs the quickest!" he says and tips his head back as he takes a sip. I've been drinking beer since I was three years old. Barker told me my mom used to dip my pacifier in it as a way to calm me down. It was Mom's go-to form of comfort and I guess she figured if it worked for her, it would work for me too.

"Ha!" I laugh. "I got you beat on this for sure." I tilt my head all the way back and pour the liquid into the back of my throat, swallowing carefully so that I don't cough. I down the entire bottle in one long swig, then jerk my head forward again. He stares at me in awe.

"That's pretty cool," he says, snapping a photo. "Can you do that too?" He turns to Mikki. She puts the bottle to her lips and starts drinking, but I know there's no way she can do it in one gulp like I can. Still, she keeps going till the bottle's empty.

John appears with another bottle for each of us and we go through the same routine again. I feel like I'm at some kind of modeling shoot and even though I never even thought of myself as pretty, I feel glamorous and grown up, drinking beer, being admired by an older guy, having my picture taken. At the end of the second bottle, I start to feel slightly dizzy and look around for my sandwich. A little food will settle me down in no time. It's not there. John must have taken it back into the kitchen when he brought out the beer.

"Can I get my food back?" I ask him.

"No problem," he says and heads to the kitchen. When he comes back in, he's got two more bottles of beer. "Just show me you can do it one more time, and the food's all yours."

Who does he think he's dealing with? Some wimp who can't manage more than two drinks? I can hold my alcohol without getting drunk. Not that I've ever been inebriated. Even though I was introduced to beer young, I'm really clear that I'll never end up like Mom. She ruined her life and almost ruined mine in the process, so even though I enjoy some alcohol, I know for sure I will never let myself get addicted.

I pause because I don't really want to drink any more beer right now. John puts the bottles down and winds his arm around my waist. "Can't do it?" he teases, and his hand feels so cool on my skin that I throw caution to the wind. I pick up the bottle and drain it, laughing a little stupidly. Mikki does the same. I catch her eye and as we stare at each other, we start giggling. I don't even know what we're laughing at but all of a sudden, I can't stop. I stumble a little and Mikki catches me. We fall into each other's arms, shaking with laughter. I think to myself that we better stop, or John's going to see us for the stupid little girls we are, but he roars with laughter.

"This is great! Even better than I'd hoped," he says, and steers us toward the sofa where we fall down in a heap on top of each other. John extricates himself and as he pulls away, his hand catches the string of Mikki's bikini top. With one pull, the whole thing comes undone, and she's sitting on top of me, her breasts almost touching my face. She puts her hand up to cover at least one of her tits, but John says, "Don't do that Mikki," and when she looks questioningly at him, he looks at me and says, "I think Kallie wants you to stay right where you are, don't you Kallie?"

A slew of emotions rip through me all at the same time. How does he know that's what I want? I've shared a room with Mikki so I've seen her getting undressed plenty of times. Quite often, I have to turn away because my groin gets all tingly.

"Keep your eyes closed," John whispers to Mikki as he moves toward her. He pushes me away so that I half fall off the couch onto the floor. I see him start to undo his pants and just like that, my mind is razor sharp.

"Get off her," I hiss. He pulls his pants down further..

"Stop!" I yell, scrambling onto all fours so I can grab him.

I want to jump him, but my reflexes aren't there. My body is sluggish, but my head is clear. And right now, the sinking feeling I had when Mrs. Clark told me we had to leave is back, and it's worse than ever.

"Don't worry," he says. "I'm not going to do anything she doesn't want. We're not going to have sex. We're just fooling around. You're okay with that, aren't you Mikki?"

She nods and smiles. I know she's gone a lot further than this with other guys. Grown-ups tell us fifteen is too young for sex, but they're lying. Everyone knows kids our age are horny as heck and that most of those adults did far more at our age than they're willing to admit. And how often do we get a chance to be with an older guy instead of some nasty teenager with bad acne and no clue what he's doing?

"Hey, I have an idea," John says and throws me the phone. "You be the photographer this time."

I can't tell what Mikki's thinking, but she's got this dazed smile on her face, so I think she must be okay and I start clicking away, like I'm some kind of professional. I get all fascinated with what I'm doing and start taking pictures of them from every angle. I feel a little bit turned on, watching him rubbing against her. She still has her bikini bottom on and he doesn't actually do anything to Mikki, just lies on top of her, getting himself worked up. In a couple of minutes he turns away, letting his cum spew on the floor, then sits back on his haunches, his limp dick dangling like a chili pepper hanging out to dry. For the life of me, I can't understand what it is about that appendage that's so appealing. It's so ugly. Especially compared to something as beautiful as Mikki's breasts.

John turns toward me and instinctively I back away a little.

"It's okay," he says. "I know a dyke when I see one." I feel a sick feeling in the pit of my stomach. I've wondered about myself for a long time, but I don't want to be gay. I just want to be normal, and fit in, and being a lesbian would be one more mark against me. I've never had a boyfriend, and never really wanted one but maybe that's because of what Mom's boyfriends did to me. If I was with the right guy, I might be fine. I decide now is a good time to put this theory to the test.

"Nah," I say. "You got that all wrong. Come over here

Romeo." He doesn't need a second invitation.

He places himself on top of me and starts shifting around but I can tell that he's not really into it that much. I can't blame him. Mikki's such a girly girl; she'd never be mistaken for a boy like I sometimes am.

"Kiss me," I whisper. He looks surprised, but he willingly puts his tongue in my mouth. I can taste the beer on it, and also stale smoke, and I feel as if I'm going to burst with pride for being with this cool guy. I pull him toward me and picture it's Mikki I'm kissing, until I realize that that defeats the purpose of being with a guy. I guess he can tell I'm not that much into it with him because he stops what he's doing and hands me the half-empty bottle of beer he was drinking before we started all this.

"Take a swig." I take a long slug and he says, "Hold on, I want a photo." I lie back, holding the bottle and tip my head back, as if I'm some kind of magazine model who's enjoying a sophisticated cocktail.

"Great!" he says and I drain the bottle. "Now, put the bottle between your legs." If I didn't have such a buzz on, I'd probably be shocked, but as it is, I place the bottle against the crotch of my shorts.. "Perfect," he says snapping away, and I feel like a Playboy model.

I can't wait to see the pictures he's taken and show them to—well I don't really have anyone to show them to. Still, I'll have them for myself and Mikki, who right now looks like she's passed out.

"Listen," he says, "I have to go out for a bit. How about you and her take showers and put on some nice clothes and make yourselves dinner." He stands up and pulls his pants up. I feel like a failure and I guess he sees my reaction.

"This was a fantastic afternoon and you're both great girls. Don't worry, the night is young; I'll be back soon."

I feel slightly mollified and start shaking Mikki. She rolls over and I pull her up.

"Shower time," I say, and once again, I feel like the mom, taking care of her wayward kid. Which makes me think of Mrs. Clark all over again, and I feel that empty space inside my chest expand. Today's been too long, and it's still not over. Up and down, up and down, like the roller coaster you see advertised at Busch Gardens, another place I've never been to. Right now, I feel like I'm on one of the rides I saw last year on the news. Kids went on this roller-coaster and at first it was great, but then it got stuck and left them all dangling in the air.

"Come on." I pull Mikki a bit more roughly than I intend. "The party's just begun. And we are not going to sleep through it."

CHAPTER THIRTEEN

I wake up, my head throbbing so badly it feels like someone's banging on it with a hammer. For a moment I can't place where I am. I open my eyes and see the red satin sheets and the vanity, and it starts to come back to me. I lie in bed, trying to remember everything that happened yesterday, but it feels like my brain will burst. I remember John taking pictures on our phones. I want to look at them to see how they make me look so I stumble out of bed and look around for my phone. My clothes are in a pile in the corner along with my backpack. I tip out the contents of the backpack but it's not there, so I get dressed then tiptoe across the hall and peek into Mikki's room. She's out cold, snoring underneath the red satin sheets. I go into the living room and am surprised to see that it's immaculate. You'd never have known anyone was even here, except for a stale smell of cigarettes, marijuana, and beer. John must have cleaned up. The bottles and joint butts are gone, and apparently so is he. In the kitchen, a couple of clean plates and glasses are stacked neatly in the dish drainer and other than that, nothing's out of place. I open the pantry to make sure all the food is there, and sure enough, the cupboard is still full. But I don't see my phone anywhere.

I decide to wake Mikki up and see if she has my cell phone. I go into her room and shake her on the shoulder. She rolls over, so she has her back to me.

"Mikki," I whisper. "Wake up."

"Go away," she mutters.

"Come on, I need to ask you something."

She pulls the sheet over her head and I figure her headache must be even worse than mine. So I go back to the kitchen. Since there's nothing else to do, I decide to have some breakfast. I take out a can of Coke from the fridge and place a Pop-Tart in the toaster. When it pops up, I go to sit on the love seat, the one where we all started doing the crazy stuff, and stare out at the ocean.

I don't know where John's gone—I still don't even know who he is—but I figure when he gets back he'll tell me where my cell phone is. I go to the front door to see if maybe he's in the hallway, but when I try to open it, I can't. It seems like it's jammed or something, because when I turn the deadbolt, it just spins around in circles without unlocking the door. I guess John will fix it when he gets back. Meanwhile, it's okay that I can't go out, since I have no idea where I am and wouldn't know how to get back in. I go back to the living room and sit down, trying to remember everything that happened yesterday, but it's all a bit hazy. I know he came back in the evening and that we hung out and watched TV. I think maybe we made out some more, but that part's real hazy because we had more beers and even though I swore I'd never smoke a joint, I'm pretty sure I did anyway. And possibly more than one.

I sit for a long time opposite the window, looking down below to where people who look tiny carry their beach chairs and coolers onto the beach. I see a car pull into the parking lot and a couple get out carrying Dunkin' Donuts paper bags. It's a long way down, but I'd recognize the Dunkin' Donuts logo and colors anywhere. After a while, I get a little bored so I pull a puzzle book off one of the shelves in the living room and figure I'll do some puzzles until Mikki gets up. By lunchtime, when she still hasn't come out of her room, I decide to go wake her up.

When I open her door, I see she's on her bed, fully dressed.

"Hey," I say. "What are you doing? Don't you want to get something to eat?"

"Leave me alone," she snarls.

Earlier I thought she was just hungover, but now I'm starting to think it's something else.

"Are you mad at me?" I ask her, still standing by the door, waiting for her to invite me in and sit on the bed with her.

She shrugs.

"Come on, Mikki, what's going on?"

She turns her head in my direction, but looks beyond me. "Aren't you embarrassed?"

"What about?"

She puts her head down. "You know…"

The problem is, I don't. I remember in the afternoon, when it was her and me and John, and yes, I do remember feeling turned on by her. Is that what she's referring to, or was there something else. Something worse?

"I don't remember much about yesterday, especially not about last night. In fact, I was thinking that if I looked at the pictures on our cell phones, it might help me remember. But I can't find my phone."

Her eyes grow big and then I see tears well up and spill over onto her cheeks.

"I can't find mine either," she gulps. At first, I don't know why she's crying and then it hits me: this is no coincidence.

"He took them?" I whisper, a very sick feeling starting to stir in my stomach.

She nods. "I guess."

I decide to risk going into her room and I go over and sit at the vanity.

"Tell me what happened last night that I don't remember," I say. But she shakes her head.

I start to mentally check my body and see if anything hurts but nothing does, so I don't think there was any violence. Before I put my clothes on this morning, I glanced at myself in the mirror and I don't remember seeing any marks anywhere, so I don't think anyone did anything perverted. I'm pretty sure neither of us had to fight or struggle with those guys though I've been in enough sex ed classes to know that if you're too drunk to say no, that's assault. I'm pretty sure Mikki isn't a virgin, so I don't think sex per se would have been an issue, unless someone made her do something against her will.

"Did he hurt you?" I ask and I know my voice is thick with concern. I've always felt protective of Mikki, and if John did something to her, I swear I'll take a knife from the kitchen and stab him with it the moment he comes through the door. I don't care if it puts me in prison.

She shakes her head.

"So what—?"

"Drop it, okay?" she says and pulls herself up from the bed. "I'm going to get something to eat."

And that's as much as I can get out of her. After a minute, I follow her into the kitchen and make myself a peanut butter and jelly sandwich. I try not to think about the fact that both our cell phones are gone and that even though those pictures were taken for fun, I'm pretty sure they could be used in some sick way if someone had a mind to. Most of all I try not to think about the fact that we are locked in, with no way of escape. I try really hard not to think about that.

CHAPTER FOURTEEN

Why am I such a sucker? That first day when she showed us around and I looked out of the window at the bay shimmering way below us, I couldn't believe my luck. I should have known that good things don't happen to people like me and Mikki. An apartment overlooking the beach, a fridge stocked with food and beer, I thought, who'd ever want to leave here?

What a joke. We want to leave. Desperately. But we can't.

The beautiful floor-to-ceiling windows don't open, so there's no way we can hang out the window and signal to someone to rescue us. Even if anyone were to look up, we're so high above them, they couldn't even see us. And if they did spot two young girls standing at a window waving, they'd probably just laugh and wave back. It wouldn't occur to them that in many ways we're as trapped as those poor girls kept for years in that run-down Cleveland dump.

We don't have our cell phones and there's no landline in the apartment. We don't have families who would know we're missing, and the couple of friends we have who might have contacted us probably just think we're being flaky when we don't answer their texts. We were going to play a tennis tournament, but when we didn't show up, I'm sure the organizers didn't think, "Wow, those girls must have been kidnapped, I better call the cops." More likely they thought, "See you can never trust fosters to follow through. I knew Mrs. Clark was wasting her time with those two."

Is Mrs. Clark behind all this? I keep trying to figure out who's the mastermind. Mrs. Clark seemed like such a nice lady. But now everything she did seems suspicious. Why did she encourage us to get rid of our old clothes? If she never took us to the beach or the pool, why did she buy us swimsuits? She said once the school vacation started, she'd take us. But instead, Parminder came and told us we were moving and then that woman told us we were coming to this condo. Were Mrs. Clark and Parminder in it together? Mrs. Clark acted like she was completely shocked that we were leaving, like she had no idea we were being moved, but what if she was just faking us out? She even had an expression on her face like she wasn't surprised. As if she knew it was going to happen. Or what if she really was shocked and Parminder's the one behind it? Parminder told Mrs. Clark that Barker ordered the transfer. But why wouldn't Barker have told us herself, before she left for wherever the fuck she was going? And who was the woman who actually drove us to the condo? She never introduced herself to us at all. Is she the mastermind?

Perhaps it's none of them. Maybe Mrs. Clark is just a loving foster mother, Parminder is the social work intern doing what she's told, and the woman who drove us here was just doing someone a favor.

Or maybe it was that woman. "Your ride fell through and we didn't want you to miss out on such a great opportunity," she said when she picked us up at the bus station. Who did she mean by "we?" Did she know what she was bringing us to? She seemed like a really nice lady, all excited for us. Was she just softening us up?

And then there's John. Where does he fit in? Is he the owner of this place? Is he the mastermind? But if he arranged it all, how did he get everyone to go along with his plan? You can't just move two kids out of foster care without a ton of bureaucracy. So he must have the blessing of Child Welfare Services. How is he connected to them? And why hasn't he come back? Why bring us here and then abandon us?

At first, I was scared of what would happen when he came back. I thought maybe he was going to drug us up and turn us into prostitutes. Maybe that *was* his plan but then something happened to him. Part of me wants him to come back, and another part of me doesn't. But what happens if the food runs out? At the beginning, we couldn't believe how well stocked the fridge and pantry were. We gorged on pizza and pasta, we ate cookies by the bagful. But now we've started to ration ourselves. Except that we have no idea how long the rations need to last. What if nobody ever comes back and we just starve to death?

Mikki would barely look at me for the first couple of days and when I tried to talk to her, she answered everything with one-word answers. But I guess at some point she realized we need to be allies. We started banging on the front door and on the walls, but nobody ever heard. I think these places mostly belong to the retired people from up north, who come here for winter. Mrs. Clark told me they're called snowbirds, but I never did understand why. All I know is that by November Pelican Bay will be full of white-haired couples, the men in their plaid shorts, the women with their pink sun visors. But by November, we could be dead. How long can you survive if you only have water?

Is anyone looking for us? There's been no mention of it on the news. How can two foster kids just disappear and nobody notices? We don't have our phones and there's no tablets or laptops here so we can't google ourselves or see if anyone, anywhere, has mentioned us. We spend a lot of time watching TV because there's nothing much else to do. I finished the puzzle book on my second day here and I hate reading so I haven't bothered look at the books on the shelf in the living room. I only read when I have to. Mrs. Clark said she was going to find out what books we needed for the new semester so we could get a head start. But then we got taken away. Or she sent us away.

I feel like I'm going mad. I have to be strong. And I have to keep Mikki strong. She spends a lot of time crying.

"What if we never get out of here? What if he comes back and starts pimping us? What if he doesn't come back?"

I pretend that I don't have the exact same fears. "Don't worry," I say. "It won't be much longer. Something obviously went wrong with somebody's plan for us. Maybe the door wasn't meant to be locked and they wanted to experiment and see how long we'd stay by ourselves. That lady who brought us here said we were having a vacation so that's why nobody's come to find us. I'm sure Barker will sort it out when she gets back. She's always had our backs."

And it's true Barker has never let us down. I've known

Barker longer than anyone else in my life apart from my mom. She used to be all timid with me, but now she's more like a favorite aunt. Not that I've ever had one of those. Problem is, because things have been going so well, she only visits us once a month and if she was out of town, who knows when she was planning on coming out again?

When Mrs. Clark got off the phone, she said Parminder was coming to get us but that the order came from Barker. I'm not sure I believe that. Barker's usually pretty good about giving us a heads up when something's going to happen.

"Remember how freaked out we were when they grabbed us out of Mrs. V.'s foster home late at night?" Mikki said, when we were trying to work it out earlier today. "Barker didn't tell us why until we overheard a social worker say they just discovered Mrs. V.'s husband had been abusing kids for years."

"Yeah, and she had nowhere for us to go and even the Receiving Home was so full we had to sleep on pullout beds in their offices."

"Barker felt so bad about us being there she said if it ever happened again, she'd figure something else out. Maybe she found out something about Mrs. Clark and needed a place in a hurry and some friend of hers offered her this condo." Mikki twists her hair around her fingers, nervously. "Maybe there's some kind of miscommunication and once Barker's back from her vacation, she'll find out what happened and come rescue us."

I nod, because I need Mikki to stay hopeful. But inside I think maybe someone purposely timed this for when Barker was away. And whoever that person is has a reason for stealing our phones and keeping us locked up.

.

CHAPTER FIFTEEN

Today's the day we have to get out of here. The food's all gone and our stomachs are starting to hurt. If we don't do something today, we're not going to have any brainpower or energy left to think of anything. It has to be today.

"There's only two ways out of here. The front door or the living room window," I say to Mikki as if we've never had this conversation before. We have it every day but today I'm not going to drop it.

We're sitting on the sofa, looking out at the gorgeous, hateful view. Mikki sits with her knees tucked under her chin, her arms wrapped around her legs. I am splayed out on the love seat, my arms and legs at whatever odd angle they fall. I'm wearing a pair of new shorts Mrs. Clark bought me and a striped tank top. Mikki is wearing the same clothes she's been wearing for three days now. I try to get her to go through her suitcase and wear something clean, but she just asks me, what's the point?

"Let's just break the window," Mikki says wearily.

"And do what? It's way too far to jump. We're not going to risk breaking our necks."

"But if we could shatter the window, someone would see us."

"What if they don't look up? Then we're stuck with a broken window letting the hundred-degree hot air in, and I don't think I could bear that. We have to break the front door down."

"How? We don't have any tools. We've tried bashing the furniture into it and it didn't splinter. We've tried jumping against it and nothing happened. It's obviously not wood, and it's obviously reinforced." I wrack my brains. There has to be some other way.

"It has to be the window," she repeats. "Even if nobody looks up when we first do it, if we can throw the glass all the way to the street, someone's gonna step on it or get a flat tire from it. That will make them look up to see where it came from."

"Why would they think it came from up here? Why wouldn't they just think someone was carrying glass into the building and smashed it?" Still, I know her plan is the best one and I think today's the day we have to go through with it. "You're right, Mikki. Let's do it. What shall we smash the glass with? We need to get big pieces to fall, not just little ones."

Mikki looks around, but then she starts shaking.

"What if he's here somewhere?" Mikki says. "What if he sees us, or hears us before anyone else does. What if he gets mad and hurts us?"

We've had this same conversation for days. We come up with a plan and then nix it because we're too scared we're gonna get in trouble if it doesn't work out.

"We don't have a choice. If he hurts us, he does. If we do nothing, we're hurting ourselves."

There's no balcony and the dividers between the windows are vertical, so we'll have to be really careful how we break them as there's nothing to stop us falling right through. We head into the kitchen to look for something to smash the glass. We realize right away that the knives and forks, the plastic spatula, the pasta server, and all the other utensils we've been using, won't do a thing.

"The microwave!" Mikki yells, and it's the most animated I've heard her voice in days. "We can throw the microwave out the window." She's right. She's so right we both start laughing gleefully.

"Not only will they see the glass, they'll also wonder where the heck the microwave came from." I tell her, "You're a genius." She looks pleased and for the first time in a week, gives me a hug. Now that I think our ordeal may be over soon, I decide to take a chance and ask her something.

"What happened that first night?" I ask as I unplug the

microwave. "What made you embarrassed to even look at me? Did I do something awful to you?"

The smile fades from her face as quickly as it came. "No. You didn't."

"Then why wouldn't you look at me?"

"Because you did do something, but it wasn't awful." Now I'm sorry I asked. I feel ashamed, embarrassed. My face feels like it's flaming red and I turn away from her. "It was what happened that afternoon and then again when he came back. I was making out with him and then he said I should make out with you so you wouldn't be left out."

"We did that and I forgot?"

She shakes her head. "He was too high to even pay that much attention. We just danced real close and acted like we were into each other."

"What part wasn't awful?" I whisper.

"The feelings you gave me. I've been with guys and had those feelings, but I never thought I'd have the same feeling with a girl."

"It doesn't mean anything…" I've been telling myself that for so long. I still don't believe it.

"I'm not saying I'm gay. I know you are but—no, don't try to interrupt. Everyone knows you're gay, Kallie, except you. I mean, look at how you dress, what you like doing, who you're attracted to. Accept it. There's nothing wrong with it. What I discovered for myself is that I may be bi. I liked what you did."

"Better than John?"

"I can't even tell you how I felt with John. I was too drunk and the day was too weird. I know I'm attracted to dudes. I just think now I'm ready to admit that I'm attracted to girls as well."

I listen to what she's saying, and I feel lightheaded. It may be because we're trapped together and starving, but it may also be that I think perhaps she's right. That I do have to accept myself for who I am.

"Barker's gay," she says to me. "Why don't you ask her what that lifestyle is like?"

"How do you know she's gay?"

"Everyone knows. Only you don't, because you're so busy denying who you are that you can't admit anyone in the whole world is gay, let alone the social worker you look up to and admire.

I dunno, maybe you even have a crush on her."

"Nah," I say, and it's the truth. "She's too old and too frumpy. Those shapeless dresses and flat shoes? That dyed hair in a style from the last decade? She's a great social worker, but I'm definitely not attracted to her. Don't take this the wrong way, but you'd be much more my type than she is."

"More than John?" she asks.

"Nothing happened with him. I thought I wanted it to, but I guess even he knew about me."

"You're a great human being Kallie. You're fun, you're smart..., and yes, you're sexy. You're gonna make some young chick very happy!"

We both laugh. "Thanks Mikki." We have a long hug and then I say, "Let's go unplug that microwave. I have so much energy right now, I can't wait to put it right through that sheet of glass."

Mikki removes the cooking tray, and then I pick up the microwave, stand a couple of feet back from the window, and hurl it at the window. It hits the glass. And bounces right off.

"What the heck?" Mikki looks at me in horror.

I'm confused, and then I remember the ads I've seen on television. "It must be that hurricane glass." Who'd have fucking thought? It looks just like regular glass and I can't believe that we won't be able to shatter it. "Let's try again. We'll stand farther back and both throw it really hard."

We swing the microwave back and forth and then on the count of three we heave it at the window. I hear the glass shatter and think, thank god. But that's all it does. It shatters but it doesn't break or fall. It stays right where it is. Mikki runs out of the room and I know she's flung herself on her bed and is sobbing. I'm too miserable to even go comfort her. I've used all my energy trying to throw the microwave, and now I feel completely defeated. I sit back on the sofa and I start punching myself in the forehead. "Dumb fuck, dumb fuck. What did you think? You were smarter than whoever left you here?"

I never seriously thought we might die here, but for the first time, I start to get really scared.

I can't let myself go down that road though. I think about Barker instead. Not the part Mikki said—I definitely don't have a crush on her. No, I think about how she's been there for me for ten years. She has to be looking for me. She must know something about what happened to us. She's smart. She can figure it out. Surely she'll come through now?

BARKER

CHAPTER SIXTEEN

June 16

I can't put off trying Mrs. Clark's house again any longer. With twenty-five families to monitor a week, and five new assessments, it's hard to make room in my schedule, especially going all the way up past Tarpon Avenue. I'm on my way to check out a potential new home, and I figure if I cut short that visit by twenty minutes, I can swing by Mrs. Clark's. I've tried calling a couple of times, but just get the same message—the number is no longer in service. With all the emphasis on client confidentiality, email is no longer considered an appropriate form of communication, so the only ways to get in touch with clients are by phone or by mail, and I don't want to put anything in writing.

I drive first to the prospective new home, a family who looks great on paper. Two older kids in college, two high-schoolers still at home. I'll have to find out where the older kids will sleep when they come home for semester breaks. Dad's an accountant and Mom does some volunteer work with the local domestic violence shelter, but mostly she's a stay-at-home. They're very involved with their local faith community, which is usually an excellent thing for foster kids, but since it's a Jewish temple, I'll have to explain that they can't be taking Pinellas County children there unless those kids happen to have been brought up Jewish.

And that's not likely since I've never had a Jewish foster kid on my caseload in fifteen years on the job.

The house looks well maintained from the outside. This time of year with all the heavy rains, everything grows like crazy, but I can see their lawn is recently cut and their bushes trimmed. My knock is answered by a short, curly haired woman who pumps my hand enthusiastically and brings me inside. I can smell cinnamon, apples, and some other heavenly aroma of baking and I think, what kid wouldn't want to live here? We go into the kitchen where Mrs. Green whips up iced coffees to go with the pastries. She tells me their name and has me try to say it.

"Arugula?" I'm confused.

She laughs. "Rugelach. Pronounce the 'ch' at the end like you're clearing your throat."

I still can't say it properly, but they're warm from the oven and they melt in my mouth so who cares? I know plenty of social workers who won't eat or drink anything when they do home visits, but I'm not one of them. My colleagues question the cleanliness of the home, or get concerned that they might offend someone if they don't like something they're offered. I figure all these homes are a lot safer than some of the cheap restaurants where we buy lunch, and I think breaking bread with someone—or in this case, rugelach—is the best way to help them relax. After all, having some stranger inspect your home isn't the easiest thing to go through.

Mrs. Green walks me through the house and I inspect the locks, the childproofing, make sure there's a closet for the child's clothes—needless to say there are plenty—and go through the rest of my checklist. Mrs. Green talks the whole time. She's funny and warm, and I think she's going to be a perfect foster mother. We sit in her living room and I ask my standard question about how she disciplines her children.

"I take away their food privileges," she says.

"Dessert you mean?"

"No. Dessert is something they have to earn with good behavior. If they've been good all week, they get dessert on Friday." I check in mentally with myself. Yes, today is Friday, hence the rugelach. "Food privileges means basic meals. If it's a small infraction, they lose a meal, usually dinner. If it's something more serious, they don't eat for the whole day."

I feel sick. Is she serious?

"You deprive them of food? What do you do, make them stay in their room?"

"Oh no, that wouldn't work nearly as well. I cook their favorite meal and make them sit at the table. Then the rest of the family eats, and they watch. It's a great way to ensure infractions never happen. When my oldest daughter was fourteen, she stayed out beyond curfew. I found out she'd gone to the movies with a boy from school. I grounded her and gave her nothing to eat the entire weekend, and let me tell you, she never did *that* again."

It's not the first time I've heard a parent proudly describe an abusive situation as if it were the most natural thing in the world, but I'm furious that it's this parent in this situation. Not only have I lost a prospective foster home, now I'm going to have to make a child abuse report which can take hours. Usually I explain to the parent why I have to make the report, but this woman is so creepy that I decide I'm not going to say a word. I ought to call the report in right now, but I really need to get to Mrs. Clark's and I'm already running late, thanks to the coffee and cake, which is now churning in my stomach as if I'd eaten poison.

"How soon will I get my first child?" she asks as I stand up. *When hell freezes over,* I think.

"There's some paperwork I have to file first. We'll be in touch," I say, trying to avoid shaking her hand as I back out of the front door.

I jump in the car and start heading over to Mrs. Clark. I feel as if I need to take a shower. I'm the first one to know that people don't have the word "abuser" tattooed on their forehead, but still, I like to think I can read people reasonably well. If you'd have told me Mrs. Green was going to turn out to be a member of the Bates Motel, I'd have laughed in your face.

***

I pull up to Mrs. Clark's domicile and right away, I see her car in front of the garage. I feel as if an enormous weight has just been lifted from my chest. When I ring the doorbell, she answers almost immediately.

"Hello Barker, this is a surprise! I didn't think I'd be seeing you for now."

I'm not sure what she means. "I couldn't get you on the

phone."

"I had to change my number. I kept getting hang-up calls and some kind of heavy breathing from a private number."

"I'm sorry to hear that," I say. "But I wish you'd have left me the new number."

"I was planning on giving it to you, but I didn't think you'd need it right away. I only got home yesterday. But don't stand on the doorstep, come on in."

As we walk down the hallway, I notice the usual clutter of tennis rackets and gym shoes isn't there. We go into the kitchen and she offers me a soda, but I decline.

"You mentioned coming home. Where did you go?"

"I took myself on a last-minute hiking trip to the Chattahoochee National Forest in Georgia. Oh my word, it was spectacular. Have you been there?"

"Georgia? You went to Georgia?" What is going on today? Have all my parents lost their minds? She can't be taking Florida foster kids hiking out of state without my permission. She knows that.

"Yes. I've been meaning to go. And after the girls left, I decided I would just jump right on it before I got the next lot in."

"The girls left...? What do you mean?" I try to sound calm but inside I'm screaming. *The girls left and you didn't call my office?*

Now it's her turn to look confused.

"What do I mean? I don't understand what you're asking." She pours herself a glass of water and sets it on the counter.

"You just said the girls left. Where did they go?" Please, let this be some kind of nightmare, and I'm going to wake up any minute.

"Why I don't know. I thought you'd know that. You arranged it."

"I—I what??"

She is looking at me like I'm mad, and I start to feel like I might just be going crazy.

"I got a call from your office. She said the girls were being moved. I must admit, I was quite disappointed. I really thought things were going so well. I had so many plans for them, I even thought—"

I don't want to hear it. "Who called? When?"

"I don't remember her name. It was while you were on

vacation. How was your vacation by the way?"

How can she make small talk with me? But then I realize that as far as she's concerned, nothing untoward has happened.

"Retreat. I went on a spiritual retreat. It was great," I say through gritted teeth. "But I don't understand how you just let the girls go."

"Hon," she says. "Being a foster parent, I just do what I'm told. The worker said you told her to pick up the girls. When she got here, she showed me her badge, so of course I let her take them. What else was I to do?" She looks at me strangely. "Is something wrong?"

I'm not sure how to answer. "Describe the person who picked up the girls. Did you check that she had a county badge?"

Mrs. Clark describes the person and I know right away it's my student, Parminder.

"Tell me again which day she came to take the girls?"

"Let me see…" She starts doing mental calculations in her head, I hear her mumbling which days the girls were scheduled for tennis. "It was so hot. I asked them if they were sure they wanted to play…but you know how young girls are, they'll play in any weather…and then the next morning, yes, the next morning—June thirteenth."

"Are you sure?"

She nods her head vigorously. "Yes, because it wasn't quite as hot and I remember thinking what a shame it was, that they wouldn't get to play tennis later that day. After they left, I felt so depressed I knew I had to do something dramatic. And right when I was looking at the newspaper, there was an article about places of beauty that were less than a day's drive away, and I thought—"

"Thanks." I cut her off because I really don't want to hear her thought process. I already have more than enough information.

Parminder Chatterjee finished her internship on June twelfth, one day before she picked up the girls from Mrs. Clark's home.

***

I call Sam while I'm still in the car on the way back to the office. He and the grandkids are back from Cape Canaveral but he's still on vacation. "I wouldn't call if it weren't urgent," I tell him. "But I have to report something pretty serious to you." I tell him what's happened.

"Go right to my office, and don't talk to anyone. I'll be there within the hour."

When I get back to the county building, I head to my desk and start drafting an incident report, although I know this is way bigger than just writing up a statement. I hate doing this kind of bureaucratic stuff. I know I'm no good at it. Sam will write the official report but he'll need my version of events to do so. When he arrives, he pokes his head around the partition and motions for me to follow him. I gather up my laptop and some notes while he strides away, making his way swiftly down the hall. In his office, he pulls out the county manual. He's wearing a dark suit, and has a dark blue tie against his stiffly ironed shirt. My heart sinks. His usual attire consists of cotton pants with a polo shirt, or perhaps a light-colored, button-down, short-sleeved shirt. He only looks this formal when he has a meeting with the Chief or when he talks to the press. In this case, I suspect he may have to do both.

I tell him again what happened.

"Why didn't you tell me the day you went to Mrs. Clark's and no one was home?"

"I didn't want to get Mrs. Clark into trouble. She's been a model foster parent."

"Didn't want to get yourself in trouble more like it," he mutters. "This is why you're not a supervisor. You don't think like one."

I bristle but tell myself that this is just fear for his own job talking. "It's true that I didn't want to get the department in trouble. I was hoping the family would come home from some camping trip they'd forgotten to inform us about, and nobody would be any the wiser."

He grunts. I show him the report I've written up so that he can see the timeline of events.

"You didn't think it odd that she'd changed her phone number and you couldn't contact her?"

"My clients change their numbers all the time. Or they forget to pay their bills so they have no phone connection for a few days. Foster parents aren't usually wealthy." In theory, we don't accept foster families unless they can prove they have enough income without the stipend they receive for having kids in their homes. In practice, many of them need every penny we give them. I don't tell him that Mrs. Clark isn't one of those foster parents living on the edge, using the county payments to make ends meet. "And you're sure it was your student who picked them up?"

"Our county isn't exactly the poster child for diversity. She's the only Asian-Indian we had on staff."

"And now she's abroad somewhere?"

"Yes. I emailed her right away, but the email bounced back with an error stating that it was undeliverable."

He looks at me with his eyes narrowed. "What address?"

"Her university one of course. It's the only one I have."

"She must have given us details of her next-of-kin from when she started her internship."

"She gave us her parents' address and home phone number. However, I distinctly remember that she told me they spend every summer in India. So we don't have any way to contact them."

"You've really messed everything up this time." Sam is practically snarling at me.

"I hardly think you can blame me for any of this," I respond wearily. I'm so tired of always having to answer to some person in authority for everything I do. I remember the days when a social worker just got on with her job. I remember when we barely had to do any documentation because most of our time was spent serving our clients instead of writing up reports and filling out billing sheets. But everything's changed in my profession and now it's all about being accountable to stakeholders.

Sam sighs at my response. "Did you document your first visit to the home, when they weren't there?"

"Not yet. I know I should have, but I just didn't get to it yet."

"Good. I don't like to do this, but since we only have twenty-four hours to report an incident, we're gonna have to make it look like today was the first day you went out there. You got behind on your visits because of your vacation." I don't interrupt him to remind him that it was a retreat to renew my batteries, one that he suggested. "It still won't look good, but it will look a hell of a lot better than not telling anyone about two missing children for several days. And I don't need to tell you that this is strictly between you and me, do I?"

"No sir, of course not."

Relief floods through me. I knew I ran the risk of losing my job over this fiasco, but now I'm not in it alone. Sam has become complicit in falsifying our documentation. If I go, Sam goes. And given how close he is to retirement, that's not going to happen. Which means when all this is over, I'll still have a job.

CHAPTER SEVENTEEN

June 20

The call comes in at two in the afternoon.

"I've got good news and bad news about your girls," Detective Gordon says. "Come to my office."

I'm so nervous, I throw the truck into reverse instead of drive and almost hit the car behind me in the parking lot. News. It's what I've hoped for, and also what I've dreaded. I roar down the highway, figuring if anyone stops me for speeding, I can toss Detective Gordon's name at them.

"Tell me," I say when I charge into Gordon's cubicle. I'm breathing so heavily, I'm panting, having taken the steps up to the station two at a time and then practically run down the corridor to his office.

"The good news is that they're alive and in good shape. Or at least they were when these were taken." He motions to a pile of papers on his desk and I realize they're photographs. I spin them around so they face me, and then I almost wish I hadn't. The first picture I see is Kallie, posing in a bikini top and shorts with a bottle between her legs. I feel sick to my stomach.

"How…?"

"Somebody mailed them to her mom in jail."

"They…?"

"I'm guessing it was the guy in the pictures." He moves the top photo to reveal several more. There's Kallie again, this time there's a man standing behind her. You can't see his face, just his arms around her. The next one is Mikki, in a bikini, with part of a man on top of her. There are several more pictures. In most of

99

them, the girls look drunk, and Mikki even looks like she may be passed out.

"But why would they mail pictures to Kallie's Mom?"

He pulls out a piece of paper and pushes it across the table. There's a message typed in large font, bold characters. "YOUR KIDS WILL GO DOWN THE SAME PATH YOU DID IF YOU DON'T LET THEM GO. SEE WHAT HAPPENS TO THEM WHEN THEY DON'T HAVE GOOD, SOLID PARENTS WHO ARE THERE FOR THEM ALL THE TIME? LET SOMEONE ADOPT THEM!"

"When were they mailed?"

"Days ago."

"Then why did it take so long for them to come to light?" I'm frustrated to think they should have been discovered so much sooner than they were.

"Because of the extra time it takes for mail to be processed in the jail."

"It shouldn't have taken *that* long," I say.

"When the mail-screening officer saw these, she put them aside for her supervisor. But the supervisor wasn't due to report for work until two days later and then the officer forgot about them. She didn't remember until some of the guards started talking about Kallie's mom after they saw the news."

"But if they were mailed to Kallie's mom, weren't they also sent to Ms. Caladesi?"

"They were. But Mikki's mom recently became homeless so we only tracked down the ones sent to her after we found out about the ones received by Kallie's mom."

I shake my head. Those poor girls. They must be so scared.

"So now what? Do you know where the photos were taken? Can you figure out who the man is?"

"That's where we were hoping you might be able to help us. Can you think of anyone who would do something like this? Sounds like this guy has some kind of gripe against women whose kids end up in foster care."

"Well that doesn't exactly narrow it down. You only have to read the letters to the editor of any newspaper to know how most people feel about people whose kids end up in the system."

"Yeah, but this seems like it's a lot more personal.

Someone who knows the girls' moms, or the girls, or someone who was in foster care themselves."

I read the message again. "Not that I'm any kind of detective—that's your job—but presumably there were no fingerprints on this?"

"Right. And we can't get any information from the printing either. We're trying to rule out people who have been in foster care. Do you know if Mrs. Clark was in the system?"

"Mrs. Clark? But that makes no sense. Why would she take the girls in and then do this? She's a great foster parent."

"Yeah, but right now we only have her word for it that someone from your office took the girls. She couldn't even give us the social worker's name. Doesn't that seem odd to you?"

"Yes, I thought that myself. But then when she told me more details, I knew it was my intern."

"And how clever is that—to choose someone who wasn't going to be available for us to check up on her?"

Everything he says makes sense. It all started with Mrs. Clark. Actually, it all started with me being out of reach at the retreat. Usually if I go on vacation, I tell my clients they can still call my cell phone in an emergency. This was the first time I've been completely unavailable to them. Mrs. Clark knew that. It seems as if with cunning planning, she could indeed have set this whole thing up. But it still makes no sense as to why she would have done so.

Then I remember a conversation we had a couple of months back.

I'm ready to adopt them, as soon as their parents give up their rights, she'd told me.

Don't hold your breath, I said. *Those girls have been in the system for years and Ms. Fergus and Ms. Caladesi have never been willing to let them go.*

"Let me see if I can do some detective work on Mrs. Clark for you. Maybe we missed something when we did our background checks on her."

"That'd be helpful." Gordon's expression belies his words. He doesn't sound like he expects me to find anything, and I realize that he spends all day every day examining records and following leads and most of them probably end up as dead ends. He picks up the photos again.

"What about this guy. Do you have any idea who he could

be? We think perhaps the girls know him."

"What makes you think that?"

"They don't look unhappy. I mean, of course it's hard to tell since they're obviously pickled, but still, they don't look scared. So we're thinking they must already know the guy."

"But they're only fifteen. Where would they know him from, assuming he's a man and not a boy?"

"Definitely an adult," he says, looking down at the pictures, and I don't ask why. I really don't want the details.

"These two kids are fairly sheltered. They go to school, come home, go to tennis, do homework, not a whole lot else. Mrs. Clark is pretty good at keeping them on a tight leash and out of trouble."

"What about the tennis club?"

"I don't think so. They only play with kids their own age. And Mrs. Clark chaperones them to and from there."

Gordon sighs. I really want to help him, and most of all I want to help get the girls out of whatever situation they're in. We both look at the pictures again. Surely, there has to be some clue there? Gordon says the girls don't look scared, but from what I can see, the place looks like a bordello. How does he know they're not being forced to smile, forced to get loaded? It's been almost a week—how many men have been there since those pictures were taken?

All of a sudden, I have an idea. "Do you think he could be a friend of Mrs. Clark?" he asks at the same time that I'm about to say the identical thing to him. Great minds think alike. Whenever I say that to Wynn she comes back at me with, "Fools never differ."

"She led a pretty quiet life when Mr. Clark was alive, but who knows what she's got into since then. Maybe something flipped." I've had my suspicions about his death all along. I never heard of anyone dying from rabies and even though I know now that it happens occasionally, I also know that if he'd had a rabies vaccine in time, he wouldn't have died. Why wouldn't she have made him get to a hospital sooner and when she did get him there, why didn't she tell someone about the bats? She only mentioned it after he was unconscious and on the ventilator and by then it was too late to do anything about it. I thought they had a pretty good relationship, but it seemed like she got over him pretty quickly. Maybe things weren't all they appeared to be. Foster families are pretty good at covering up stuff they don't want us to know.

"Will you bring her in for questioning?" I ask.

"I definitely want to talk to her again. Last time it was pretty brief. What I'd like to do is go out there with you. Less threatening than if I bring her in here. And if you're with me, she's less likely to think about wanting an attorney." Gordon puts the pictures back in the envelope. "Will your workplace give you the time to do that?"

"Sure," I respond. "We need to do whatever it takes. Sam's looking after a couple of my cases for me. We can go first thing tomorrow." I can't wait to hear what Mrs. Clark has to say. I think back to last week's home evaluation with the weird and evil Mrs. Green. Perhaps I'm not such a good judge of character after all. What kinds of secrets does Mrs. Clark hold?

CHAPTER EIGHTEEN

The next morning when I enter Gordon's office, I can tell something good has happened. His desk is clean and Gordon himself looks ten years younger.

"The girls are out," he tells me getting up from his desk. For the first time in all the years I've known him, he gives me a hug. Then he picks up the car keys.

"Are we still going to Mrs. Clark?"

"You betcha. Now more than ever I want to talk to her."

As Gordon and I drive to Mrs. Clark's house, I ask him to tell me everything he knows about the girls.

"I don't know that much yet. I was only allowed to speak with them briefly, after they'd been checked in at the hospital."

"Are they okay?"

"The hospital was just precautionary. They'll keep them overnight then probably release them tomorrow morning."

"How did they escape?"

"Another anonymous note. This time it was put in a janitor's mailbox. I still have to interview him, but I don't expect he's gonna be able to tell us much. The officers who responded to his call said he didn't seem to know anything about the owner or the renter. He's just on-call for problems with plumbing and the like."

"And the girls, how did they seem?"

"Like you might expect typical fifteen-year-olds to look— as if they'd known all along they'd be okay. But I'm pretty sure it was all bravado. Underneath I could see they were pretty shook up. Especially the one with the long, dark hair."

"Michaela."

"Yeah. They both asked if you were responsible for finding them. Guess they're pretty tight with you."

"I'm the only person they've had consistently in their lives for the past ten years. I can't wait to see them and talk to them."

"You'll have to let me interview them first. And that won't happen until tomorrow when they're released from the hospital."

"But you've done an initial interview?"

"Yeah. I wanted to get some basic information to see if it would move us forward with our investigation. But tomorrow I'll be talking to them at length."

"Could I be there?"

"No. I promise I'll pass them on as soon as I'm done."

"Did you find out anything useful today?"

"Yeah. Mrs. Clark told you that the girls were picked up by someone from your office, who you later figured out was your student. The girls corroborated that—Kallie even remembered her name. But here's the strange thing. She took them to the bus station. It was someone else who drove them to the condo."

"Do they know who he was?"

"It wasn't a 'he,' it was a female. Drove an older model white KIA Soul. Guess Kallie's enough of a car expert to know how it differs from the newer models."

"Oh, even I know that car. Wynn drives a white KIA Soul, and hers is an older model too."

"Wynn? Your partner Wynn?" He swivels his head around to look at me and his eyebrows are raised almost to the roof of the car.

I laugh. "I don't mean—of course, I don't mean she had anything to do with it! I'm just saying, I know that exact car." Gordon says nothing. "Come on! You don't seriously think…"

"Of course not," he says and quickly changes the subject. "Is this where we turn off for Mrs. Clark?"

***

Mrs. Clark has baked brownies and offers them to us, but after the fiasco with Mrs. Green, I decide I'm done accepting dessert from clients. Gordon has no such inhibition and happily takes a large corner piece, which he breaks into chunks as he takes a sip of the coffee Mrs. Clark has offered us. Unabashed, he dunks a piece of brownie into his drink and asks, "What exactly did Parminder Chatterjee tell you when she called to say she was removing the girls?"

We are in the dining alcove and Mrs. Clark is sitting on the edge of an upright chair at the table across from Gordon. She pulls her skirt down over her knees, nervously, like a prim schoolgirl. "As I told Barker, she didn't tell me anything."

"And you didn't think that was odd? You didn't try to argue with her, or ask to speak with a supervisor."

"I did think it was odd. But I've been at enough meetings of foster parents to hear about things like this happening all the time."

"But why should something like this happen to *you*? You knew there was no chance of the girls being reunited with family." I can't stop myself from blurting out the question. There is something surprising about the ease with which Mrs. Clark handed over the girls, considering how close she was to them.

Gordon drums his fingers on the table. "Uh—I'll ask the questions, Barker, if that's okay with you." I realize I overstepped my bounds, but my blood is pumping too fast. I decide to get up and walk into the living room.

The sectional sofa is neither new nor worn out. It is brown corduroy, practical, the ideal furniture for kids who might spill things on it. Across from the sofa is a faux fireplace and above it a mantelpiece with a row of photographs on it. They all feature Mrs. Clark's deceased husband. There's a picture of him with a rifle slung over his shoulder, and I turn away from one in which he's holding up what is obviously a trophy pair of antlers. Mrs. Clark isn't in those pictures, though it's hard to know whether she was the photographer or if it was someone else. In the center is a large framed picture with dates beneath it, so it must be the one she used for the memorial service. By then the press had found out how Mr. Clark died and were all over her, so she kept the service very private and didn't want anyone from the county attending. The photograph shows Mr. Clark in a dress suit with no hint of a smile.

Of all the photos, there's only one picture of the two of them together. It's obviously from several years ago and looks like a family celebration of some kind, with balloons in the background. He was taller than her and has his arm around her protectively. I've never met anyone from her family and don't know who came to the memorial. When I looked at her original application last night, there was a checkmark next to the box that asked about children. Apparently, she has two grown-up kids. She's never mentioned them and it seems odd there are no photographs of them. I never saw her original foster parent application and the social worker who approved the Clarks isn't with our agency any more so I don't know what the story is with that.

I wander back into the dining room, having calmed down a lot. Mrs. Clark is telling Gordon about her husband's death, although I'm sure he read about it in the newspaper.

"Kallie and Michaela were such a comfort to me at that time. They were unbelievably mature in how they handled everything," she tells him. I sit back down. Gordon looks at his notebook then pulls something out from between one of the pages of the book.

"You must have had friends who supported you through that terrible time. Do you mind if I ask who your close friends are?"

She pauses. "I'm embarrassed to say, I don't really have many friends. I guess I'm a bit of a loner."

"What about dating? I know it hasn't been that long, but have you started to see other men yet?"

"Oh no. Seth was it for me. I'm not going to get involved with anyone at my age."

Gordon smiles sympathetically. "You're not that old."

"It's not about my age. I just couldn't go through all those awful dating routines."

Gordon pulls out the paper he's had in his hand for a few minutes and I see that it's one of the photographs that was mailed to Kallie's mom.

"Do you know this guy?" he asks.

This is the whole purpose of our visit and he's worked up to it with subtlety.

Mrs. Clark puts on a pair of reading glasses she has on a beaded lanyard around her neck, and peers at the photo. She shakes her head. "I don't think so, but it's not very clear. Do you have any others?" She doesn't seem shocked to see the girls, but when Gordon pulls out another one I see that he's had the pictures cropped so that neither of the girls is in view. She looks again. "No, I'm pretty sure I've never seen him. Why? Is he connected to the girls' disappearance?"

"I'm not at liberty to say," says Gordon, and I think that surely just by saying that, he is telling her that this man is indeed connected. "Do you think Kallie or Mikki might have had the opportunity to meet with men while they were living under your roof? Did they ever sneak out in the evenings? Or say they were going somewhere and later you found out they hadn't?"

Again, Mrs. Clark shakes her head. "No. They're both fairly introverted. I think they preferred playing games on their phones to going out and meeting new people. They're only fifteen. I don't know if they're even interested in dating yet, although perhaps that's just me being old-fashioned." Gordon puts the photographs away and scribbles in his notebook again.

Mrs. Clark plays nervously with her hair, twisting it around her finger back and forth.

"Those earrings are lovely," I tell her, and she moves her hand over to her ear, feeling the earring as a way to remind herself which ones she wore that morning. I've done the same myself, many a time when people compliment me on my jewelry. "Did you make them yourself?"

"I did. Remember you said I needed to do something outside of my routine? You suggested a jewelry-making class and I found one up near Clearwater. You were right; it was great, although unfortunately we only had a couple of sessions."

"How come?"

"I don't know. The others just dropped out. It was a shame because the teacher, Wynn Larimer, was a lovely woman."

"Wynn Larimer?" Gordon looks up from his notebook and turns to me. "Isn't she your—?" I flare my eyes wide and give a little shake of my head to stop him. I keep my private life private, and Mrs. Clark doesn't need to know anything about it. He corrects himself quickly. "I thought perhaps she'd been your teacher as well," he says quickly.

"Do I look like someone who would make jewelry?" I say and we all laugh. Even though I wear some of the stuff Wynn makes, I'm not big into adorning myself.

"So, what made her such a nice woman, this teacher of yours?" Gordon asks.

"She was very easy to talk to. She and I had a long chat after the first class. We even discussed the whole foster care system. She had pretty strong views about it, as I remember."

Gordon perks up again. "Like what?" he asks.

"She seemed to be pretty pissed off at the birth moms. Thought we foster parents were letting them off the hook."

"Hey Barker," he turns to me. "Any chance you could, uh, step outside for some fresh air?" I raise my eyebrows, knowing that the temperature is almost 90 degrees and the last thing I want is fresh air, but I know when I'm not wanted. I have my suspicions that he wants to ask some more questions about Wynn, although perhaps it's something else he heard that he wants to follow up on. Whatever it is, Gordon's smart. He'll figure it out.

CHAPTER NINETEEN

June 22

I've been sitting on this hard bench waiting over two hours for them to release Wynn. Every time the steel door opens, I get up and open my arms, ready for her to fall into them, and each time some other person walks through instead, my heart sinks. They're only allowed to keep her for twenty-four hours if they don't charge her and we're already at twenty-three, so she has to be out soon.

I've spent plenty of time here professionally. I lost count of how many times I came here to pick up clients when I worked with Family Preservation. Usually, they were women I'd been working with for months, helping them manage all the tasks they needed to complete to get their kids back, reassuring them that they could make it and be successful parents. Then right when they were about to be reunified with their kids, they'd do something stupid, like get arrested for public intoxication. It was almost like clockwork, and it made me wonder whether they really wanted their kids back. All my hours of counseling them, supervising their visits, advocating with attorneys and other social workers, to say nothing of the endless documentation, would all go down the tubes. That's why I decided to leave that side of the department and work with the foster families instead. Not that all of them are perfect, but at least I don't spend hours sitting at Central Booking and when I'm at the courthouse it's usually for a good reason like a finalized adoption.

Sam has assured me that I can take off as much time as I need to get this all sorted out. I'd like to think he was being kind, but I can't help wondering whether he just wants me out of the way. After all, it's my partner who is being accused of kidnapping my clients, and that doesn't exactly paint me in the best light. But there are certain pieces of unfinished business I'm still going to have to stay on top of. I pull out my smartphone and start checking my work email. I've been in the business long enough to remember when we had no mobile phones. First they gave us flip phones. It was a struggle to get the county to issue smartphones to people who weren't in management, but once they realized how much more productive it made us, all of a sudden they couldn't hand them out fast enough. I scroll down and read that Cindy's likely to be out on sick leave for an extended period of time. Poor Sam, now he's down two people, both senior social workers. It doesn't say what she has, so I start composing a tactful email to ask what's going on. It's probably related to her elderly father, though I hope it's not about her or one of her children. I'm engrossed in writing the email when suddenly I feel a little tap on my shoulder.

"Barker?" I jump up to see Wynn standing at my side, looking about as forlorn as a person can be.

"Honey, I'm so sorry," I open my arms ready to embrace her, but she just looks at me and says, "Let's get out of here."

It seems to take all of her strength just to climb into the cab of the truck and my heart goes out to her. "I bought your favorite ice cream," I tell her, hoping to cheer her up. "We can eat the whole tub in one night if you want."

"You think that's going to solve this?" She looks at me like I've gone mad.

"Of course not. I just wanted you to have something to look forward to when you got home."

"I know, I'm sorry. I'm just tired and cranky."

We drive away from the jailhouse in silence.

"Barker." She turns to me. "What's going on?"

I feel my stomach give a little jolt. "What do you mean?"

"Why is this happening to me? None of it makes any sense."

"We'll get to the bottom of it." I've always been able to comfort Wynn when she needs it, and reassure her. With one hand on the steering wheel, I pat her knee. "Don't worry."

She turns her whole body in the seat, practically coming out of her seat belt. "What is wrong with you, Barker? They suspect me of kidnapping two fifteen-year-old girls. They implied that if they have enough to charge me, there could be other charges as well, even more serious, though God knows how anything could be worse than that." Obviously, no one has told her about the photographs. I wonder why they withheld that part from her. "Did you at least get me an attorney?"

"I don't think we're there yet, sweetheart. Let's just get home, you can relax, and we can talk. I have some ideas about how we should proceed with all this."

She turns back to face front. I glance over, see that she's looking out the window into the distance, and wonder if she's imagining what it would be like to lose the freedom to drive down a road lined with coconut palms, blood-red hibiscus and spreading oaks dripping with Spanish moss. But it won't come to that, I know it won't.

When we pull up, Queen and Latifah come racing to the door to greet her, their tails wagging furiously. For the first time I see a smile on her face as they lunge toward her, Queen jumping up and down and Latifah standing on her hind legs and wrapping her front paws around Wynn's waist.

"Did you miss me girls?" Wynn leans to the left to pet Queen at the same time as she runs her hand through Latifah's thick fur.

Once inside I make her a cup of strong tea and cut a large slice of pound cake to go with it.

"Tea time!" I announce. Wynn has told me repeatedly that when she was a child her Viv always said, "There's no problem great or small, that a cup of tea doesn't help solve." Even in ninety-degree weather. She washes up and we sit at the kitchen table.

"Now," I command. "Tell me everything they told you."

"First of all, they told me the girls had been found. But they didn't tell me anything else about them. They must have told you what happened?" She cocks her head to one side, like Queen does when she wants to know why I haven't given her a second treat after her walk.

"I only found out the girls were safe yesterday morning, just a few hours before they arrested you. Someone got the janitor to check up on the apartment. Before that, the only thing I knew was the other day when Gordon called me into his office. He said that someone had sent pictures of Kallie and Michaela to their moms, and he showed them to me."

"He had pictures of the girls? And you didn't tell me?"

"Honey, the whole thing is confidential. You know I can't tell you about my clients and Gordon told me not to tell anyone about the photos. He showed them to me because it was part of his investigation. It's not like I knew they were going to arrest you and you'd need to know any of this. I figured when they found the girls, then I could tell you everything because it would be in the papers and everyone would know."

"Why did they send pictures? Were they trying to get a ransom? Did they think someone had money to pay them?"

"No. They wanted to shock the birth moms. The pictures were…well, I guess I should tell you even though he told me not to. The pictures were sexual."

"*What?*"

"It's hard to know what actually happened. The photos were very suggestive poses with the girls and some guy. If something did happen, it might have been consensual. I'm not naïve, I've had the talk with Mikki who's admitted she's no innocent. But even if she wanted it, since the girls are only fifteen, it's statutory rape at the very least. I won't know until I get to see the girls and talk to them but with you being the one who was arrested, I don't know whether I'll be able to talk to them. If I can't, I'm sure Gordon will keep me in the loop."

"Is Gordon the one who arrested me? The mean guy?"

"No. I guess because we're friends, he sent someone else. He didn't question you when you were in jail?"

"It was the same two who picked me up, the mean guy and the younger woman."

"They must have told you their names."

"There was no way I was going to remember them, so I didn't even try."

I had a feeling this would happen, that Wynn wouldn't be able to hold onto important details. She takes a big gulp of tea and picks at the cake.

"Wynn, did they tell you why they thought you were connected to all of this?"

"Apparently I took the girls to the condo."

"You…but you never said anything to me. Why on earth wouldn't you have mentioned it when you knew they went missing?"

"I didn't know it was them. She said I was taking two eighteen-year-olds who were aging out of the system."

"Who's she?"

"Parminder, your student. We have to track her down. She can sort everything out for us."

"Mrs. Clark also told me that Parminder was the one who took the girls. But we have to wait until August to get in touch with her. She's volunteering somewhere abroad for the summer, and we don't know where, or with whom."

"But she must have a phone number or email?"

"The only email address I had for her was her university one. I emailed her but it bounced back. I guess she switched her phone off because she's out of the country. But she'll be back for the new semester, so at least we know we can talk to her then."

"But August might be too late! And if she's really involved with setting this whole thing up, who knows if she really went abroad or if she's really coming back?"

"You think Parminder master-minded this?"

"She called Mrs. Clark, and she called me. She knew you were out of town. And then she heads out somewhere that no one can contact her? There's no way all of that is coincidence. Surely the cops can see that and find her?"

"I'm sure they're trying. They were actually more focused on Mrs. Clark."

"Yeah, they brought her up in my interrogation."

"Interview, sweetheart, you're not in Guantanamo." I try to lighten up the mood, even though I know this is heavy, serious stuff.

"It sure felt like I was. You have no idea how much they were pressuring me to confess."

"What did they say about Mrs. Clark?"

"They asked about a conversation we had. Of course I couldn't remember any of the details, but she said I made some weird comments about how birth moms need to be taught a lesson. Which is pretty fucked up, coming from her."

"What do you mean?"

"Well, she was a birth mom who lost her own daughters. I mean, I know it probably wasn't her fault..."

"Wait! What do you mean she lost her own daughters? She

had kids in foster care? She never mentioned that to us. And it never came up in her security clearances."

"No. Nothing like that. Like I said, I don't remember all the details of our conversation, but I certainly remember her telling the whole class that she had twin daughters who died of meningitis. That's not something you forget."

"My God, Wynn, I had no idea! I can't believe she withheld that from us."

"But wouldn't that be something you find out when you do background checks?"

Sometimes I forget how people who are outside the system really don't know anything about it.

"They're done through the FBI database. They look to see if people have arrest histories, that kind of thing. If there was nothing suspicious about her daughters, it wouldn't come up in any kind of background check."

"Well I think it's pretty damn suspicious she didn't tell you she lost twin daughters, and yet she told a bunch of total strangers."

"That *is* weird."

"In fact, I remember her saying she must have blurted it out because she so rarely talked about it. Why would she keep it secret?"

"I don't know. Maybe because she knew that if we thought she were using foster kids as a way to replace her own, we might have thought twice about placing children with her. Although, the fact is, we're so damn short of homes, it probably wouldn't have even made a difference."

"So what will you do? Can you talk to her? Can Gordon?"

"I'll definitely ask him to look into it."

Wynn puts her cup down and squirms in her chair trying to get comfortable. Her eyes are sunken and hollow and she looks exhausted. "Why don't you draw a bath and put in some of those relaxing bath salts you have? I can order us a pizza and we'll spend the evening snuggling up together. There's nothing else we can do tonight, so let's try and take our minds off everything."

I see her facial expression go through a number of different permutations. I know she wants to keep talking about all this, but there's no point. It will just keep her worked up and we won't gain anything. And the last thing I want is for her to start ruminating on all the small details, going over and over everything in her mind and getting frustrated. So I take advantage of the fact that she'll do anything not to upset me. I take her cup and saucer and put them in the sink.

She sighs. "I guess you're right, but…"

I steer her gently toward the bathroom. "No buts, sweetie. Time to relax."

She looks at me and shakes her head. "I don't think there's much chance of that until my name is cleared and all this is just a bad dream."

WYNN

CHAPTER TWENTY

A Week Earlier

"Is this Wynn?" The voice on the other end of the phone is a little breathy and has a slight accent.

"That depends who's calling."

"This is Parminder, Barker's student. I'm sorry to bother you, but I need you to do us a favor." I thought Barker told me Parminder's last day was yesterday, the same day Barker left for the retreat, but I'm hardly one to hold on to details like that. "We have a fantastic benefactor who donated his beachfront condo for two weeks. He wants us to give it to two foster kids who are aging out of the system. That means they've reached the age of eighteen, so we don't have to provide homes for them anymore." I remember now what Barker said about Parminder. That she's very condescending and comes across as a know-it-all. Does she really think I don't know what it means for kids to age out of the system? "We just heard of two girls for whom this would be perfect. I'm already on my way to pick them up but I have a plane to catch so I can't take them to the condo. It's in Pelican Beach."

Shit. I was really hoping to get some jewelry finished for the juried competition I've entered. It's the first time I've done anything like this and with Barker being away, I thought I could just focus exclusively on getting something really beautiful and dramatic created. In fact, I was planning on putting the phone on silent, but of course, I forgot to. Driving to Pelican Beach and back will take over two hours out of my day.

"Can't they get a taxi?"

"Right now, the county is still responsible for them. I need to set up the ride. These poor girls. I can't even tell you what they've been through. It would be such a shame if they couldn't get to the condo—"

"I'll do it," I interrupt her. I don't need all the details. All the kids have been through a hard time, thanks to their damn mothers. And aging out of the system, that's awful. I've heard people minimize aging out by comparing it to joining the army, or getting married, but that's totally different. Eighteen-year-olds who do that have the support of the military or their families. They don't just get dumped on the street. If these girls can have the vacation of a lifetime, who am I to prevent it? "Go ahead and give me the info."

"The owner's name is Damien. And he doesn't want them to know that he's the benefactor. So when you meet him there, just tell the girls he's a friend of yours. He said he has an errand to run, so if he's not in the condo when you arrive, he'll leave the door unlocked."

"Anything I need to know about the girls?"

"We want to surprise them. So don't give them any information until you get there. They're both shy, so it's not worth trying to engage them in conversation. By all means, tell them how great Pelican Beach is, and what a great time they're going to have. It's hard to believe that even though they live in North County, some of these foster kids never get to go to the beach." *Oh Parminder, you're so green. When you've been in the business as long as Barker, nothing will be hard to believe.* "I'm so happy you're going to do this," she continues. "No one deserves a break as much as these two."

"Happy to oblige. So you're off to catch a plane?"

"Yes, I'm going on an amazing adventure, it's—" I hear a noise, like a car door slamming. "—I have to go. I just pulled up at the house. Oh, and since you're connected to Barker and it might look a bit odd you taking on this errand, don't tell them who you are, okay?"

***

I told Parminder I'd meet her at the bus station and would

be there to pick up the girls before she had to leave, but of course, it ends up taking me longer to get myself organized than I expected. As usual, I haven't yet taken the dogs out, so I have to run them around real fast, and this is one of those mornings when Latifah takes forever to decide where she's going to make her deposit. Parminder told me if she couldn't wait for me, the girls would be on a bench opposite the bus station. Sure enough, as I pull up I see two young girls sitting demurely on a bench. They're both medium height, one has short blond hair and the other has dark black curls that cascade down her back. Blondie's wearing cutoff shorts and a ripped tank top. She's all muscle and I can't help thinking she looks like a very cute baby dyke. Curly is a little taller, and is wearing a striped sundress. Surprisingly, they're both carrying tennis rackets along with their suitcases. They look like true vacationers and I'm so happy for them. I look at their scuffed suitcases and wonder whether these are all the possessions they own, or whether someone is storing more of their stuff. I try to think back to what it was like to be eighteen and starting out alone in the world, but I was never alone. Yes, I went off to college, but I knew my mom was just a phone call away. What would it be like to go to college and never have a home to go to at Thanksgiving, never have a parent to call in time of need?

I open the trunk for their belongings and they fling them in. They both look so young, it's hard to believe they're eighteen. Then again, that's the problem with getting older. Everyone looks so young, even my doctor looks as if he's barely graduated high school.

I drive them over to the address Parminder gave me. I'd love to get into a conversation with them—find out where they'll be going after this, ask them if they're glad to be aging out of the system, or scared—but I remember Parminder's instructions and keep everything simple, reiterating what a great time they're going to have in this condo.

When we pull up, I see it's an older high-rise building that has probably seen better times. But it overlooks the water, so the views must be stunning. Rich foliage surrounds a very private entrance around the side of the building. If I owned a beachfront condo, this is definitely the type I'd want. Not one of those newer ones with grandiose entryways that demand keypad entries just to get inside and have slimy doormen who pretend they're there to help you but really they're just keeping tabs on who's coming and going.

The girls and I go up to the eleventh floor. I'm as excited as they are to see the condo. They chatter excitedly and when we open the front door, they can't believe their luck.

They look at me in wonder.

"You deserve this," I tell them. "This is going to be an experience you'll never forget."

CHAPTER TWENTY-ONE

A Week Later

"Tell us why you did it," the Mean Cop says, leaning forward on his elbows, his shirtsleeves rolled up above them.

I sigh. "I don't even know what 'it' is. Why don't *you* tell *me* why you brought me here?"

I look around, although there's nothing to see. The room is a windowless box, with just enough space for a table and three chairs. The walls are a dull beige with nothing on them at all. Mean Cop is sitting opposite me, a digital recorder in front of him on the table. Young Cop is sitting on my side of the table slightly behind me. The whole place is so completely depersonalized that I've decided from now on I will think of them only by initials: MC is Mean Cop and YC is Young Cop. I will pay no attention to their appearance and make them faceless and nameless.

"You know why you're here," MC says, and I am reminded suddenly of an incident with an ex-girlfriend years ago, long before Barker. One day she came storming home and started madly throwing her clothes haphazardly into a suitcase.

"I am so outta here!" she yelled. "What did you think? I wouldn't find out?" I saw her take a blouse that I knew was mine, but I didn't dare say anything.

"Find out what?" I put my hand on her arm to try to stop her from packing so she would tell me what was going on, but she spun around and almost hit me in the face as she jerked her arm away.

"Don't touch me!" She kept yelling and swearing while I kept begging her to tell me what I'd done.

"You know perfectly well what you did," she spat out as she jammed her suitcase shut. The next day she sent her best friend over to pick up the rest of her stuff, and I never heard from her again. To this day, I don't know what I did, if in fact I did anything at all. Now MC is doing the same thing.

"I believe it's my right to know why you brought me in for questioning." Hopefully my voice sounds more confident than I feel.

"Do the names Michaela Caladesi and Kallie Fergus mean anything to you?"

"Of course. They're Barker's clients, the ones who are missing. Have they been found?" Now I'm the one leaning forward. "Oh, do tell me they've been found."

He shakes his head, as if he can't believe what he's hearing.

"They've been found all right. Though why you would want that is beyond me."

It sounds as if he thinks I'm involved in their disappearance, and that's just bizarre. I sit and wait for him to ask his next question. He says nothing.

From behind me, I hear YC clear her throat. "Let's back up a little shall we? First of all, how did you sleep?"

The way we're seated I have to face either MC, or YC, but not both. I've heard that expression good-cop/bad-cop so many times, but I never knew how true it was. YC was the one who gave me a cup of lukewarm coffee (did they think if it was hot I'd throw it in someone's face and burn them?) and held my arm as I lowered my stiff body into the chair I now occupy. I turn to face her.

"My body was aching all over, but I have to admit that I had a better night's sleep than I've had in months. Recently I've been plagued by nightmares, and last night I didn't have any."

"Maybe there was a part of you that wanted to be found out. It must be a relief to know you don't have to carry the secret anymore." Her face shows caring but her words are painting me just as guilty as MC.

"Look, I'm not trying to be difficult. Trust me, I want this to be over a lot more than you do. But seriously, I just don't know what you guys are talking about, so why don't you tell me?" I say the words to her, but swivel around to face MC because clearly he's in charge here. But it's YC who answers and her words are so shocking I can't even believe I'm hearing them.

"We know you paid for the condo the girls were found in."

"*What?*" I'm completely aghast and then I chuckle because it's so outlandish that it's clearly a mistake.

"You think it's funny?" MC growls at me.

I turn to him. "It's not funny, but it is ludicrous. How did I pay and why would I do that?"

"We don't know why you did it, that's what we're here to find out. But as to how you did it—you wrote a check for a month's rent."

"*I* did? *I* wrote a check? That's not possible. Somebody else must have taken my checkbook. I can't even remember the last time I wrote a check." I start to feel relieved because clearly, this is all a big mistake and once they find out who really wrote the check, I'll be in the clear.

"We know you wrote the check." MC sounds tired, like maybe he didn't have much sleep, and he's been working too hard. But I refuse to feel sorry for him. "You don't remember writing a check for $1,500 to Summerlicious?"

Another relief. "Sure I do. That *is* the last check I wrote. But what does that have to do with the condo?"

MC drums his fingers on the table. "Look, we can do this the easy way, or we can make it really difficult for you." He shoves his fingers through his hair in exasperation and I feel like doing the same. What does Barker's summer program have to do with this? MC gets annoyed at me when I don't answer his questions, but he's just as annoyed when I do, so I'm starting to feel frustrated.

"I'm the one who waived my rights to have an attorney present. Why would I do that if I did whatever it is you think I did?"

"People waive their rights all the time. They think if they call an attorney it's an admission of guilt."

"Or maybe it's just because I'm so obviously innocent and this is all so blatantly a mistake?" I counter.

"We know you took the girls to the condo. Did you think we wouldn't find that out too?"

"I took the girls to the condo? The only girls I took to a condo were two eighteen-year-olds who were aging out of the system and being given a free vacation. The missing girls are only fifteen. I never met them."

"So you admit you took two girls to a beach condo in Pelican Bay?"

"Yes, but—"

"You admit it." MC leans forward so close to me that I can smell his breath, which is extremely unpleasant. Who has garlic first thing in the morning? "You admit you took the girls to the condo. So why not tell us everything else? How you set it up, what the goal was, why you did what you did."

"But I'm telling you—the girls I took were eighteen-year-olds. Ask Barker. They're not the girls you were looking for. And I took them because Barker's intern asked me to do her a favor."

"Really." MC says, but it's a not a question. It's a statement of his incredulity. "The same intern that we can't track down because she's in Guatemala. How convenient."

"I would say it's bloody inconvenient—at least for me. But it happens to be the truth." I swivel around in my chair to face YC, hearing all the bones in my neck crack as I try to turn and face her. "Please," I say, because I'm starting to feel a little worried. "Can we just get Barker in here? She'll corroborate everything I'm saying. She asked me to write the check. Well, she didn't ask me to, but she told me about the fund and when I said I wanted to give money to it, she didn't discourage me. And it was her intern who asked me to pick the girls up because she'd run out of time."

I think that she might feel some sympathy for me, but instead she asks me, "What's your connection to Mrs. Clark?"

"The girls' foster mother? I've seen her name in the newspaper, but I've never met her."

MC bangs on the table and I jump. "Why do you insist on lying to us? Do you think we're stupid? Don't you think we might just have done a little investigative work before interviewing you?"

I'm getting a headache, and I want to cry. But I won't give him that satisfaction.

"She has memory problems, remember?" YC mutters to MC, loudly enough that both he and I hear her. "Maybe we need to jog her memory." She turns to me. "Do you remember teaching a jewelry class in Clearwater in May?"

"Sure. I do, but we only had a couple of sessions because all but one of them dropped out."

"Good." YC smiles at me encouragingly. "And who was the one who didn't drop out?"

"Ava."

"And what was Ava's last name?"

"Oh gosh. I had a roster, but I don't remember..."

"Then I'll jog your memory." MC is back in charge. I swivel to face him. "It was Clark," he says, as if I've known that all along and was just toying with him, "Ava Clark."

"Right." I say. And then I hear the significance of the last name. "Of course! She said she was a foster mother. But I never dreamed she was the same one whose kids have gone missing."

"You didn't know? But you were quite friendly with her, right?"

"I wouldn't say friendly exactly. We went out for coffee after the first class. And then again when no one showed up for the second class."

"And she told you she was a foster parent?"

"Yes."

"And do you remember a conversation in which the two of you discussed the foster care system?"

"Umm..." I try to remember back to our chats. I know they were lively, but that kind of talk tends to go in one ear and out the other with me. I have to be selective about what I hold onto, and a conversation with a new possible-friend isn't likely to make the cut.

"Let me refresh your memory. She told you that she thought foster care was a bizarre system because most of the kids come from poor families and it would make a lot more sense to pay birth mothers to look after their own children instead of paying wealthier families to look after other people's children."

"That sounds vaguely familiar," I say, though honestly, I still can't really place the conversation.

"And what did you tell her?"

"I have no idea."

"You said something like, 'I guess it's to teach them a lesson. They wouldn't learn anything if they were paid to look after their own kids.' Is that right?"

I'm still not sure, but I shrug and nod a little.

"And then you said something like, 'But really it doesn't teach them a lesson when they get good foster parents like you. It lets them off the hook. If we really wanted to teach them a lesson, we'd put their kids in harm's way and let them see what happens then.' Didn't you say that?"

"Honestly? I don't recall. I can see how I might have. I mean, I don't have a lot of sympathy for the birth parents. Sometimes when I listen to some of Barker's tales, I do think the system seems like it's broken and it needs some kind of radical fix. But I still don't see what this has to do with these two girls and why you think I had anything to do with their disappearance."

"No, I'm sure you don't. But you see, we also have a copy of the letter you sent to their parents. And the sentiments in it are awfully close to the ones you voiced to Mrs. Clark. Add to that the fact that you asked Mrs. Clark all about the two girls she was looking after, right down to whether they were attractive or not, and we have a pretty solid case."

And that's when I start to get scared.

CHAPTER TWENTY-TWO

I've been trying to remember all the things Mean Cop said were proof that I kidnapped the girls. Once I can remember what they are, I can go through systematically and refute them. I think I've held onto most of it, but it feels like I'm forgetting something important.

First of all, he said I took Kallie and Michaela to the condo, which I did, although I didn't know it was them, and I was just doing Barker's student a favor. So one thing I have to do is track down Parminder. There has to be a way to find her. Surely, Barker must have discussed with her exactly which program she was going to apply for? I know how she is with her supervisees. They tell her they're thinking of doing some program somewhere and she researches it to death and comes up with five reasons why a program that she found would be ten times better than the one they picked. Then she'll track down someone she knows in the field who can give the student a sure way in, or at least a strong recommendation. She's made a lot of comments this year about not liking her student so perhaps she didn't go to all the trouble she usually does. Wouldn't that be just my luck? Still, I have to find a way to locate Parminder, preferably within the next few days. She's the only person who can explain why I took the girls to the condo. That's number one on my list.

Then there's the issue of what Ava told them about me. This I find a little bizarre. I only met her twice and I thought we got on pretty well, even though neither of us ever pursued a friendship after the class disbanded. I remember we talked about foster care, but this whole idea that I thought we should teach the birth moms a lesson, I don't remember saying that. And then there's the claim that it was important to me to know whether her foster kids were attractive. I might easily have asked her if the girls were pretty. But what's so sinister about that? Could she be the person who's setting me up? Could she have masterminded this whole thing?

It seems to me that Mrs. Ava Clark was purposely trying to point the finger at me, and the only reason I can see for doing that, is if she wanted to redirect the attention from herself. And why would she need to do that if she's completely innocent? I don't believe she is. There is definitely something suspicious about Mrs. Clark. She's had way too much tragedy in her life. And while I might feel sorry for someone who lost her spouse and daughters, I also have to wonder what the likelihood is that a person's immediate family is struck twice by such rare forms of death? Barker says Ava never even told the county about her daughters. Why not? This is definitely something I have to look into.

There's another thing that's odd about Mrs. Clark. She doesn't seem like someone who's borne tragic losses in her life. You wouldn't look at her and think, *that woman bears a heavy burden.* My class was only a few months after her husband passed. From what I know of grief, when you've had one loss it's bad enough. But when you have a second one, it tends to get compounded by the first one so that the loss of her husband would have triggered an even stronger grief reaction than would be usual. How could you carry on providing the kind of structure and nurturing that foster children need in that situation? You'd think that when her husband died, she'd have asked to have the foster children removed from her home. Who could deal with such a terrible loss like that with two foster kids around?

But why would she have had the girls kidnapped and put in the situation Barker described? She already had the girls in her home. If she wanted to pimp them, she could have done it under her own roof. And if she just wanted them to have a good time with a couple of guys, she could have arranged that too. And why would she want to do any of that?

If, for some bizarre reason, it was Ava, why would she set

me up? She barely knows me. Did she know I was Barker's partner? I was careful not to mention it, but we've never hidden our relationship from anyone, so it wouldn't be hard to find out. Oh my god! Is that why she came to my class? Because she knew I was Barker's partner and it was the perfect way to set things in motion? Is that why she mentioned her daughters, so that she'd have an excuse to talk with me afterward?

The only reason I can see for her setting me up is if she had a vendetta against Barker. But why would she? Barker was the one who placed the kids with her. If she didn't want them, she could have said no. The whole thing is extremely puzzling.

Another thing I wonder about is why the police didn't tell me about the photographs. They did say that they had a letter they thought might have been from me. But why not tell me what was going on with the girls? Is it because even they can't come up with any plausible reason why I would have wanted to set the girls up in some awful bordello situation? Or because they know I have no reason to crusade against birth moms?

So the two things I have to do right now are find Parminder and research Ava Clark. The best way to do it is probably to use the Internet. I could ask Barker to help me, but she's so involved with work and looking after me, that I don't want to put any more on her plate. I'm the one who should do it. I can set aside creating jewelry and make researching this case my full-time job. If only I were more adept at using the computer. And then I remember that Dot works in information technology. I know I've always found her intimidating but I'm pretty sure she'll help me if I ask.

I used to know her phone number, but for the life of me, I can't remember it. I go to our phone book, find it, and dial it. When she answers, it occurs to me that she may not even know about the arrest.

"Dot? Did Barker tell you what's going on with me?"

"What do you mean?" She sounds wary. I don't know why.

"Did she tell you I was arrested?"

"*No!* What on earth did you do?"

"I didn't do anything," I respond. "It's crazy. They think I took those two girls—you know the ones who were in the newspaper? They were Barker's clients. They said I took them.

Which I did, but not the way they think I did. And now they're accusing me of kidnapping!" I'm aware that I may not be making a whole lot of sense, but I'm sure, under the circumstances, it's not surprising. "I need to do some research. Someone set me up, I'm sure of it, and there are two people I need to find out a whole lot more about."

"Have you asked Barker to help you?"

"No. I don't want to mention any of this to her. She has enough on her plate. But I thought you'd be the perfect person to help me because you work with computers all the time."

"Yes, but I'm a systems manager," she says, as if that explains anything. I've never understood what she does, and I'm not about to get into it now.

"I know, but you definitely know a whole lot more than I do about researching on the Internet. All I need is some basic information about the best way to go about finding out what I need to know. Can I meet with you at your workplace? During your lunch hour or something?"

She hesitates. "Surely if this is something serious, Barker and the police are doing their research?"

"I don't know what the police are doing. They seemed pretty convinced I'm their woman. As for Barker, she told me they're totally short-staffed at work and now she has to cover for another employee, as well as take care of her own cases. I don't want to burden her. I know she's doing whatever she can from her end, but I have to do something. You have no idea what it was like, spending a night in jail.."

"You spent a night in jail? I had no idea! Why didn't Barker call us?"

"I don't imagine there was anything you could do. But there is now, and that's why I turned to you."

"I understand. Let me check my calendar." She pauses and I picture her looking at her appointment book, until I remember that nowadays most people have their schedules on their electronic devices. "I have an opening this afternoon around three. When you arrive, let the receptionist know it's a personal appointment with me, and she'll send you up." I feel an enormous sense of relief. Dot is so smart, she'll help me.

"Don't worry Wynn," she says. "We'll sort all this out."

My chest feels tight as the tears start to form in my eyes. I have to believe her. The alternative is too frightening.

CHAPTER TWENTY-THREE

Dot was great! I was afraid that when she started showing me how to do things on the computer I'd space out, or just not understand, but she made it all really simple. She had me practice things with her, and she typed up some instructions for me, so I feel pretty confident now that I can do my research.

I get home and immediately set myself in front of the laptop. When Barker comes home, she looks shocked to see me working on it.

"I decided it was time to join the twenty-first century," I tell her, but I close it down because I don't want her to see what I'm looking at. I head to the kitchen to make dinner just as the phone rings. Barker picks it up and listens to the voice on the other end. She looks a little alarmed, nods a few times then says, "Why don't we come down there right now?" She hangs up the phone and turns to me.

"The cops want to interview you again," she says.

"Why?"

"I don't know. But they asked if you could come down to the precinct now, and I said yes. I'm coming with you. This time I'll hear everything they have to say and make sure you don't say anything incriminating."

"How could I do that, when I'm completely innocent?" I get up from the desk and go to fetch my purse. As I pass her, she pulls me into her and gives me a big hug.

"Come on." She picks up the keys and we head downtown. As we drive, I realize I'm shaking. The last time I was being driven down here, I was so scared. Once I was there, it was even worse: the fingerprinting, the picture taking, the endless waiting, and then being told I was going to have to spend the night there completely freaked me out.

"What if they lock me up again?" I say, my voice thin and reedy.

"They won't," she pats my knee reassuringly, the other hand steadying the wheel. "They can't. You're out on your own recognizance. That means until the court hearing, which isn't going to be for ages. And by then they'll have figured out it's not you."

"You're sure they can't take me back?" I hear what she's saying, but it's as if a part of me can't take it in. Even though I have moments of clarity, mostly everything is starting to overwhelm me.

We arrive at the station and Barker strides down the hall while I trot nervously behind. She's been here many times with clients, so it doesn't raise the same emotions for her that it does for me. She seems to know where she's going and stops in front of an open door.

"Here," she says, pulling me in. The officer sitting behind the desk isn't one I know. "This is Detective Gordon, honey." Ah, so we're meeting with her friend, not with Mean Cop or Young Cop. I feel a sense of relief.

He stands up and pushes forward a large, hairy hand for me to shake. "Pleased to meet you," he says. "And don't worry— you don't have to say the same back. I'm sure you'd rather not be here." I like him right away. He has a firm handshake and feels like someone I can trust, as well as being someone who knows what he's doing. His office is a mess, just as I'd expect a busy law enforcement office to look. His desk is covered with a pile of papers, on which sit a coffee cup with the logo, 'World's Greatest Dad' and a half-eaten bag of potato chips scrunched up.

"I just need a few bits of information so I can square certain things away. Barker, do you want to get us something to drink from the coffee machine?"

She looks at him, a little startled. "I'll stay right here, thanks."

"Sure, fine." He looks unruffled and turns to me. "When you had your initial interview with Officers McNab and Carrillo, they brought up the issue of the check you wrote."

That's what I've been forgetting! How could I have

forgotten such a central piece of information? "Yes. They said I paid for the condo. But that's nonsense."

"And yet you admitted that you wrote a check for $1,500 to Summerlicious, which is the name of the condo owner's account."

"Then it must be a coincidence. The check I wrote was to Barker's program." Detective Gordon turns to Barker and raises his eyebrows, waiting for her to confirm what I just said. Her brow knits in puzzlement.

"Honey, I——" she looks awkward, like she is about to say something she doesn't want to say.

"I asked you if I could make a donation." I remind her, then I turn from her to Detective Gordon and explain. "Barker's workplace decided they wanted to start a fund so that foster kids could attend summer enrichment programs. I asked her if we could make a donation. She said she couldn't because of her position, but that I could make one out of my business account." I turn back to Barker, "So that's what I did, right?"

She looks embarrassed. "You did make a donation to the program. But it wasn't that check."

I'm stunned. It has to be that check!

She swivels to face the detective. "I take care of our finances, even Wynn's business account. So when she asked me to make a donation, I went to the website and used her credit card. Then I logged it in Quicken so we'd have a record of it."

"But isn't your program called Summerlicious? Isn't that what you told me?"

"Does that sound like a name we'd give to a social services program?" She smiles, but there is absolutely nothing humorous about all this. Although there's definitely something funny going on.

Detective Gordon looks a little embarrassed too. "Do you remember mailing the check?" he asks me.

I shake my head. "I put it in an envelope. But I have no idea what happened after that. I presume Barker mailed it."

"You probably did give it to me," she confirms. "Whenever Wynn or I have something that needs mailing, I take it to work and put it in the mail there. It's more convenient than going to the post office and the only mailbox near us is in an awkward location that you have to make a U-turn on a busy road to get to. So most likely I was the one who mailed it."

"Do you by any chance remember mailing something for Wynn at the end of May?"

"Wynn still does a lot of stuff by mail that other people might do online—she orders jewelry supplies, sends greeting cards and letters—so I take mail in all the time. Anyway, what difference does it make, if she acknowledges that she wrote the check?"

"I just need to cover all my bases, and I'm trying to look for any way that Wynn might be off the hook."

"Trust me, I wish I could help you." Barker's eyes fill up and I know my decision not to have her do more research with me was right. This is really wearing on her.

"What else did you want to know?" I ask. I just want to get out of there.

"Do you remember that we told you the person who took the girls sent a letter to their parents?"

Barker butts in. "I know we just told you Wynn writes a lot of letters but that's not what we meant!" She looks indignant, and I'm glad I have her here with me. Even though I don't like what we've covered so far, I feel more at ease than when I was by myself with Mean Cop and Young Cop.

"No, I wasn't barking up that tree. I wanted to talk about the substance of it. You see, we did have to do a little snooping into your background, Wynn, and we noticed something that seems pretty relevant to this case."

"I can't imagine what," I say with way more bravado than I feel because I realize the shit is about to hit the fan.

"It may be nothing, but being given away when you were two-years-old might just make you pretty angry toward birth mothers."

Barker looks dumbfounded. "Adopted? You're adopted? Why on earth didn't you ever tell me?"

"What was I going to say? That my birth mom tried me out for a couple of years and then decided to dump me?"

People who aren't adopted have no idea what it does to you, knowing that you weren't good enough to keep. When I was young, I used to tell the truth: that my mother had two small children already and that after she had me, she got so overwhelmed that she decided to keep the other two and give me away. "But didn't she ever ask for you back?" they'd ask. Or sometimes even, "Were you colicky?" I knew what they were doing—blaming me. They knew I wasn't good enough to be kept. That's when I realized I didn't need to tell anyone anything, and I just let everyone assume my mom was my birth mom.

"I'm sorry Barker," Detective Gordon says. "It was one of the reasons I thought it might be better to meet with Wynn alone. People always seem to have skeletons in their closets, and I didn't know if this might be one of Wynn's." I keep my head down.

"Is there anything else you need to know? Wynn and I can deal with our personal issues later," Barker says through gritted teeth. But I see her shaking her head from side to side. I know what she's thinking: I really do have a grudge against birth mothers. I have a secret I never told her. I'm pretty sure she's wondering what other secrets I have.

CHAPTER TWENTY-FOUR

I have been checking out Ava Clark on every possible website I can find. There are plenty of articles about the death of her husband—dying from rabies is unusual enough that not only does it make headlines in local newspapers, but it also finds its way into newsletters on health and wellness, animal welfare, and all kinds of articles about hiking, nature, and the outdoors. All the websites stress the importance of early intervention; rabies is completely curable if treated before symptoms appear. None of the sites find anything suspicious in the fact that Mrs. Clark only told the doctors about the bats after it was too late.

I discover that when people with rabies go to the hospital, the symptoms often look like something else, such as the flu. Mr. Clark went to the hospital with shortness of breath and excessive sweating and chills, which are similar to symptoms of heart disease. Since he'd had some heart problems in the past, he was transferred to another hospital where his cardiologist had admitting privileges. A few hours after his arrival at the new hospital, he stopped breathing and was transferred to the intensive care unit, where he was put on a ventilator for several days. His condition worsened, and his organs started to fail. At this point, they started doing additional interviews with Mrs. Clark, and in the course of those interviews, she mentioned that the previous year, while she and her husband were staying in a rustic cabin on a kayaking weekend they had seen bats fly through the bedroom. She was sure neither of them had been bitten by the bats, but apparently, you can be bitten when you're asleep and never know it happened. Mr. Clark's doctors sent samples of his skin and saliva to the CDC to be tested for rabies. The tests came back positive, but it was too late to administer the vaccine to Mr. Clark, who died several days later.

On the one hand, it all sounds completely above board. And on the other hand, you'd think someone must have asked Mrs. Clark something that could have triggered her thinking about the bats in the cabin a whole lot sooner. What makes it suspicious to me is the death of her daughters. It's too much for one family. So I start to research that part of her history. But that's where my Internet search draws a blank. Death from meningitis is also pretty rare, yet I can't find any website that mentions anything about two sisters dying from it. I google every possible combination of words to find a headline or article that would match Ava's description, and there's nothing. I decide that maybe they were children from a previous marriage and have a different last name, but still nothing. Is it possible that their deaths were kept under wraps? That they never made it into any newspaper or public news outlet? I don't know enough about epidemiology, but I'm pretty sure that death from bacterial meningitis would have to be reported to the CDC and would have to make it to the public eye. So why can't I find anything?

I decide to try a different tack, and just look up everything I can find about Ava Clark. The first place I look is Facebook, but I can see immediately she doesn't keep that updated because it still lists her as married. She also only has twenty friends, which even I know is way below average. So I decide to focus on the twins and start to look things up the way Dot suggested. Almost immediately, I hit the jackpot: a blog by a certain April Clark entitled, "Why I don't talk to my Mom anymore." I click on the link, my heart thumping hard. It's a short entry, explaining that sometimes the healthiest thing to do when you're in a dysfunctional family, is to cut ties. She doesn't say what the dysfunction is and keeps the focus on herself and her personal growth. That in itself wouldn't prove anything, but in the article, April mentions her twin sister, Astrid, who agrees with her decision. The fact that they're twin sisters, the fact that they won't speak to their mom, and their unusual names, also starting with 'A' all seem to me pretty damning proof. They have to be Ava's daughters! And if they are, then the story she made up about them dying from meningitis is a complete fabrication.

Later that evening, after we've had dinner and I've cleaned up, Barker and I snuggle on the couch together, watching yet another edition of a home improvement show. Barker loves those shows, and I don't mind them, although sometimes people act like such spoiled children it annoys me. During the commercials, I ask Barker if she remembers what I told her about Mrs. Clark and her daughters.

"Yes, of course. You said she told you she had twin daughters who died. That was really shocking to me, so the first thing I did when I got to work was check her file. She checked a box saying that she had no children living at home, and another box stating that she had two children living out of state."

"And no one ever interviewed those children?"

Barker laughs. "Do you know how many social workers we have in the county who do foster care home evaluations? Me and Cindy, and if we're lucky our interns once they've been trained. That's it. We interview everyone who lives in the home where the kids might be placed, but there's no way we'd have time to interview other family members. We get a pretty good sense of the foster parents when they go through our classes, and we get three letters of recommendation from non-family members like friends and clergy."

"But that's crazy! If they can pick and choose who recommends them, they'll only give you the names of people who will give them glowing reports. Surely grown kids would be the best indication of whether someone's going to be a good foster parent?"

"Not necessarily. Sometimes people parent other kids much better than their own. Remember when Dot and Evie told us how much better they are as grandparents than they were as parents? It's the same thing with foster families. They don't have the same emotional investment that messes up the relationships in their family of origin. Anyway, no one's disputing that Mrs. Clark was a perfectly good foster parent."

I wonder whether to tell her what I found out, but right then she yawns and says, "Do you mind if I have an early night? I had a really hard day today and I'm exhausted."

***

The next day, after Barker's gone to work, I call Detective Gordon.

"You said I could call if I thought of anything that might help the investigation. Correct?"

"Absolutely. What's going on?"

"Mrs. Clark told you about a conversation we had in which I said birth mothers ought to be punished. And she also said I was really interested in whether her foster daughters were attractive, right?"

"Uh-huh."

"But you have only her word for that. I mean, obviously no one else could tell you about a conversation that was just between the two of us, but hopefully you can see that she could just be making the whole thing up."

"What makes you think she would do that?"

"The reason we had that conversation was because she was concerned she'd been inappropriate in class. A class member mentioned that she was dealing with carcinoma meningitis, a form of brain cancer and Ava blurted out that her twin daughters died of meningitis." I wait for him to say something—does he know she has twin daughters? Does he think they died, or does he know they won't have contact with her? But he stays silent so I assume he wants me to carry on.

"But the point is, although she has twin daughters, they never died of meningitis. I found out they're alive and well and they just don't talk to her."

"You found out...? Why are you investigating Mrs. Clark?"

"Because I think she may have set me up. Don't you see? She makes up a story to gain my sympathy, so that afterwards she can have an excuse to talk to me. That if she ever gets asked about our conversation, she can make up stories about what I said to her."

"But why would she do that?"

"I don't know! Maybe she has something against Barker, or me, or lesbians! I only know there's definitely something suspicious about her, and I hope you'll look into it."

There's a silence on the other end of the line. Eventually, Gordon says, "I don't know how to say this tactfully, so I'm just going to say it. What you're saying, well, it sounds paranoid. I'm guessing she doesn't like to tell people her daughters don't talk to her."

"But why bring them up at all? We weren't even talking about people's kids!"

"I don't know. Lots of people don't tell the whole truth about their situations. You did the same thing—never told Barker you were adopted."

"That's different!"

"Look, I know you're struggling with some mental health problems—"

"No! I *don't* have mental health problems. I have a few issues around my memory, that's all. I'm not crazy and I'm not paranoid." I take a deep breath. I have to get him to see that someone framed me. "The other person who may have set me up is Parminder Chatterjee. She's the one who picked up the kids from Mrs. Clark and then asked me to take them to the condo. Why is no one trying to track her down? How hard can it be?"

"We're working on it, but to be honest, we don't see how she would be involved in all of this."

"Then that's even more reason to look into Mrs. Clark!" I'm trying really hard to keep my cool. What I want to do is scream and yell. It's all very well for him to treat this like it's just another investigation, which to him it is, but this is about *me*. The rest of my life depends on them finding out the truth, and they don't seem interested in doing it. In fact, based on this conversation, I'm horribly afraid that they're pegging it on me because they think I'm a crazy person.

I'm even more afraid that I may just turn into one.

CHAPTER TWENTY-FIVE

There has to be a way to contact Parminder Chatterjee. She's the one who sent me to the condo. I thought she was under orders from Barker, though whether she specifically mentioned Barker, I have no idea. Because she's her student, I just assumed we were doing the transport on her behalf. Since Barker didn't order the transport, that puts Parminder front and center on the list of suspects. It's not clear to me why the police aren't focusing on Parminder, but it seems it's up to me to find her.

Barker said Parminder went to Central or South America, so I decide I'll just contact every single program that offers internships to social work students. There can't be that many. I'll work from north to south, which means I'll start with Mexico even though it's actually in North, not Central America.

The first program I find is in Chiapas. I could imagine Barker might have encouraged Parminder to go there, because it's a place we wanted to go ourselves. It always sounded so romantic, full of revolutionaries and quaint villages. I open the laptop, confident, thanks to Dot, in my ability to do the necessary research. When I met with her, Dot explained how to download and use Skype, and, talking of revolutions, I discover that there has been a telecommunications one while my back was turned. I knew everyone was into cell phones, but what I didn't know is that you can now call anyone, anywhere in the world for free. How crazy is that? I remember the MCI calling cards we always made sure to take with us when we traveled, how we had to find a phone booth and then dial a long string of numbers to be connected to the international operator, and then another long string of numbers to actually talk to the person we were calling. Now, all I have to do is get their Skype address, and bingo, I can call them. I'm not too nervous about the language barrier since I'm the one who's always kept my Spanish skills up for when we travel.

I'm counting on the fact that the people I call in these Latino countries will not have the same kind of confidentiality hang-ups Americans have. I'm hoping that they won't tell me they can't give out any information, but that instead we'll chat and they'll be more than happy to impart everything they know. The first place I call is the Chiapas Project in Ocotopec.

"*Bueno.*" The lady facing me on the screen is tiny and dark-skinned, clearly one of the indigenous population. I've written down what I want to say so I can ask my questions without stumbling over tenses or pronouns. I explain that I'm looking for a social work student to whom I need to give a very important message.

"No," she replies, after I give her the name. "*No es un voluntario con nosotros.*" Her swift reply and willingness to give me information raises my hopes and I successfully contact several more charities and organizations in Mexico, although unfortunately all with the same result. I spend the next two hours calling organizations in Belize, which yields me nothing. I'm aware that I'm not hitting every organization because they don't all have Skype and they don't all answer, but this is the best I can do, and I'm checking off a lot of names on my list nonetheless.

If I'm going to have any hope of putting together my booth for the art show, I shouldn't be spending hours on end researching Parminder Chatterjee, but I don't feel as if I have a choice. If I'm not in jail by the time of the show, I may not have enough pieces, but if I do end up in jail, then it's really not going to matter how many pieces I've completed.

When Barker arrives home, I've worked my way through half of Guatemala. I know it's a needle in a haystack, but I have to keep trying.

"Not doing your jewelry?" she asks after flinging the heavy briefcase she schleps around with her into the hallway closet.

"It's hard to be creative, when I'm still fixated on not going back to jail." I try not to sound bitter. Sometimes Barker acts oblivious to what's going on, as if I'm not at the edge of a precipice. Her way of dealing with all of this is to ply me with tea and dessert. Today she's brought home my favorite cranberry and almond cake, so I make steaming mugs of tea and we go to sit on the back porch. When Barker first met me, she couldn't understand how I could drink hot tea in the middle of a humid, sultry summer's day. But now she's as addicted to it as I am.

"Talking of not going back to jail…I was thinking that we ought to prepare for the worst." She puts her mug down and reaches across the white wicker arm of my chair to touch my hand. It was silly of me to think she's not aware of what's going on. I guess she doesn't always know how to bring it up. It's one thing being a counselor to other people, another to do the right thing with your own partner.

"You know how even though we hope a hurricane will never hit this part of Florida, we always prepare for those tropical storms, just in case?" Barker says. "I think we should have all our legal ducks in a row, in case they come back and march you off to jail again, and this time you don't get out so quickly."

I'm shocked. How can she be so practical? How can she talk so calmly about this? She knows the whole thing is nonsense. Doesn't she?

"Is there something you know about this case that you're not telling me? Did those girls say something to implicate me even more than I'm already implicated?"

"I don't know anything." She shakes her head vigorously. "Gordon interviewed them after they were found."

"How did they get out? Gordon must have told you."

Barker tells me that somebody hand-delivered a note to the building manager suggesting something was going on in condo 1118 and that he better check it out. When he did, he found Kallie and Michaela. I ask why they hadn't been able to get away and she tells me they were locked in and had no means of communication, that someone took away their cell phones. When I press for more details, she says she doesn't have them because she hasn't actually seen them since the abduction.

"I only know what Gordon told me when he first informed me they'd been found. I thought I'd be able to talk with them as soon as the cops were done, once they were released from the hospital after they were checked out."

"And didn't you?"

"No. Once they'd been interviewed, that led to you, and after that I was out of the picture." She sounds put out, as if this is my fault.

"But they're your clients. They must want to see you."

"I'm sure they do. I've been the one looking out for them for the past ten years. I'm their connection to each other and to everything they've done in their lives. But Gordon's adamant, at least for now."

"I still don't understand how they knew I was the one who drove them there. Parminder told me to be vague so I don't think I even gave them my name."

"They weren't blindfolded. They saw the car you picked them up in, and they saw you."

"But there are a gazillion white Kia Souls on the road. Out of all the drivers, how would they have come up with me so quickly? It makes no sense."

"Honey, I don't know. But that's not what I wanted to talk about. I wanted to talk about being prepared for whatever may happen next." I'd forgotten that this is how the conversation started. I take the last sip of tea in my mug and eat the last bite of cake. I start to blot the crumbs on the plate, so as not to miss a single one.

"I think you should sign over a power of attorney to me," Barker continues. "It'll serve two purposes. Firstly, if you do end up in jail, I can make financial decisions for you, manage your business and do anything else that needs doing. Secondly, if at any point in the future, your mental health deteriorates and you're not able to make decisions—and I know we're miles away from that—everything will be in place already."

My stomach plummets, like an elevator in a New York skyscraper that just lost its cables. Getting my mom to give us power of attorney over her was a massive struggle. She'd become pretty paranoid and was convinced that Barker and I were out to steal her money and lock her away in a state hospital. Mom didn't have that much money to begin with, and I'd already seen how her unsuspecting nature had led to unscrupulous people taking advantage of her. I didn't want to see her lose any more of it so I begged her to give me the authority to manage her affairs.

Eventually she agreed, but only after bitter arguments and tantrums.

Our relationship was never the same after that. We'd be sitting in Mom's room at the nursing home, reading a book together and suddenly she'd turn to me and say, "I know why you wanted my money. You want to spend it all on that woman you live with." Even when she'd forgotten all kinds of things from the past, she remembered that. And now it's coming back to haunt me. If I refuse this request, I will become just like my mother: paranoid and untrusting. And yet...I don't want to give Barker power of attorney. It's not a case of trust—I trust Barker implicitly. It's about giving up my independence. It's about admitting that there's a chance I may end up losing my freedom, whether in jail or in my head. And I can't do that. Not now, not yet.

I say nothing. I don't need to explain it to Barker. I'm sure she can see it written all over my face. She leans forward and takes my hand. "Honey, you know I wouldn't use it unless I had to. It's a precaution. Like writing a will, which we always say we're going to do, but still haven't. It's like taking out insurance. Just something responsible people do, to stay responsible."

I know she's right. I know it. But I can't do it. I feel the tears starting to trickle down my face. And I know, more than ever, that I have got to find Parminder Chatterjee.

If I want to keep my freedom, she is the key to it.

***

When Barker tells me she needs to go out for a late meeting, I feel relieved. The moment she pulls out of the driveway, I jump back on the computer. Guatemala is two hours behind us, so I still have a couple of hours I can make calls. I pull out my list and find the next number on it. I bring up the organization on the screen so that I know who I'm going to be talking to in case I need to make polite conversation. I'm so immersed in what I'm doing, I don't even hear Barker until she's practically standing on top of me.

"Forgot my office key," she says, holding it up to show me. "What are you up to?" she asks, leaning in to look closer at the screen.

"Nothing." I feel my face redden as I click to minimize the

147

screen and bring up the wallpaper instead.

She laughs. "Whatever it is, I'm glad to see you're not pining away for me." This time she leaves for good, and I begin making my calls. On the fourth one, amazingly, I hit the jackpot.

"*Sí, está en nuestro programa.*" Yes, the faceless voice tells me, she is indeed in his program. *Yes? I've found her?* Thankfully, he has chosen not to make this a video call otherwise he might see my face turning every shade of every color as I move from excitement to fear to relief. "*Podría decirle, quién llama?*" He wants to know who's calling. I am so shocked, my heart is racing faster than Usain Bolt winning the 100-meter sprint. Now that it's happened, I'm not sure how to respond. If I say my name is Wynn, will she come to the phone? Should I say Barker instead?

I hedge my bets and tell him it's someone from the university.

"*Estará aquí mañana por la tarde.*" Tomorrow afternoon? She won't be there until tomorrow afternoon? How can I wait until then? I ask if he can be sure to have her by the phone and tell him I'll call back the next day. He confirms the time with me and I hang up.

When Barker returns, I'm just putting the clasp on a necklace made up of dangling, red, glass chili peppers.

"Those are cute," she says. "Glad the creative muse returned."

I smile. I can't wait to have my Skype conversation tomorrow with Parminder, and then share with Barker everything I learn.

CHAPTER TWENTY-SIX

I am having difficulty understanding Parminder Chatterjee, and it's not because of her accent, or because we have a bad connection. It's because what she's saying makes no sense.

I spent my day in a tizzy of anticipation, trying to create jewelry but mostly screwing it up as I dropped beads all over the floor, cut myself with my pincers and put clasps on backward. In the end, I left the jewelry and decided to make a complicated Lebanese dish I saw on the cooking channel instead. But I couldn't concentrate on that any better than my jewelry. Finally, I decided to take Queen and Latifah on the longest walk they've had in weeks, even though it's over ninety degrees outside. When we got back, I couldn't wait any longer and I clicked on the Skype icon. I got right through to the man I'd spoken with yesterday. This time answered with the video. I could see the desk he was sitting at and behind him a wall, filled with photographs of smiling children in various poses.

"*Aquí tiene,*" he said, and as he disappeared from the screen, a dark-skinned young woman replaced him.

"Hi. This is Parminder. Who am I speaking with?"

"Uh…I'm Wynn. Barker's partner."

She looks startled. "I thought Señor Rodriguez told me someone from the university was calling."

"I guess that's my bad Spanish. Sorry if I worried you."

"I wasn't worried. I was excited. I didn't get my first

choice of placement and I thought perhaps they were calling to tell me it had come through after all."

"Maybe it still will. Or you'll find that the placement you did get turns out to be really interesting. Barker told me that she didn't get the placement she wanted her second year, but that it worked out well because she ended up learning a lot about a population she might otherwise never have worked with." I'm babbling but I don't know how to start our conversation. Luckily, Parminder does it for me.

"May I ask why you're calling me?"

"It's about those two girls you asked me to pick up."

Her eyes grow big and she looks scared. "That was weeks ago. They were meant to wait for you opposite the bus station, on the park bench. Weren't they there?"

"Yes, yes. They were right where you said they would be. But there's been a bit of an issue and I just wanted to clarify a couple of things."

"What do you mean, 'an issue?'"

"After I took them to the condo, they went missing—but they're back now," I add quickly to reassure her.

"I don't understand why you're the one calling me and not Barker. I can't really talk to you about them because of confidentiality." She sounds a little pompous and I begin to understand why Barker didn't care for her.

"I'm not asking for any confidential information. I only want to ask you who it was who asked you to pick up the girls."

Parminder raises her eyebrows. "Barker of course, who else?"

And this is why what she's saying makes no sense. If she initiated the abduction, I would expect her to lie. If Mrs. Clark did, perhaps she would make up a story to cover for her too. But it makes no sense to involve Barker. Obviously if it were Barker, she'd have told me herself.

"Barker asked you?" I repeat, because I can't think of what else to say.

She nods. "She said it was an emergency. She had to have a county worker pick them up and no one except me was available. But I didn't have time to take them where they needed to go, so I should have you collect them."

"But why didn't she just call me directly instead of having

you ask me to pick them up?"

"She was at her retreat and wasn't meant to be using the phone and because you have a standing appointment on Wednesday mornings, she knew she wouldn't be able to get in touch with you right then."

My head is spinning and my brain feels so thick, I can't think. I don't have any standing appointments. Why would Parminder make this up? The only reason I can think of is that she did indeed organize the whole thing and now she's trying to put it back on the county.

"Why did you tell me the girls were eighteen?" I decide to see what else I can find out from her.

"Because they are. They wouldn't have been allowed to go to that condo if they weren't aging out of the system. It was all done in a rush because of the emergency situation. They had to be moved..." she pauses. "You'd have to ask Barker why. She said I couldn't tell you because it was confidential."

Someone clearly wanted to dupe me. I had to think the girls were eighteen because if I'd known their real age, when word got out that two fifteen-year-olds were missing, I'd have made the connection. But who is that someone? It must be Parminder and yet it doesn't sound like it was. If it's not her, why is she covering for them? I try to think what else I can ask her but she starts to speak again. "Wynn, what's going on? Why did you call? I don't even know how you found me here."

"I did a lot of digging. Why does it bother you? Are you trying to hide? I know you haven't been answering your phone or your email—"

"I didn't bring my phone, the roaming charges would be way too much, and I had to close my university account because I was getting endless spam, some of it very obscene. My family has stayed in touch via my personal email address, so if someone really wanted to find me, all they had to do was contact my parents."

"Barker told me your parents go to India every year."

"Well...that's true."

"It seems to me, you've gone out of your way to be unavailable. And the fact that you're trying to pin this on Barker makes me mad. I'm not stupid and nor is she. She had no idea those kids were being removed."

Parminder starts to look very annoyed. "Of course she knew, since she initiated it. Maybe she just wasn't allowed to tell you. I don't like being accused of lying and I'm sorry I told you anything at all. You're clearly calling behind Barker's back and I don't believe she's been trying to find me. If Barker wanted to call me, she could have called me here. She knew where I was."

My heart starts pounding. She has to be lying, she has to be. "She didn't know which program you went to," I say, though I can hear no conviction in my voice.

"Of course she did. She's the one who found me the placement. She sent another student here three years ago. And if you don't believe that then ask Señor Rodriguez. Would you like me to put him back on?" She turns around, presumably looking to see if he's still in the room, but my shaking hand has already clicked the red icon to hang up.

I sit and stare at the blank screen. It can't be true. If Barker knew where Parminder was, why didn't she tell the police? There's only one reason. She didn't want the police to find Parminder. And the only reason for that is because Barker wanted to keep the suspicion focused on either me or Mrs. Clark. I want to believe it was Mrs. Clark she was trying to frame. But I know it wasn't. I know because I was the one who wrote the check for the condo. And even though she denied it, I know Barker told me to write it. Barker has been lying to me all along.

Suddenly, I'm shaking violently. My stomach seizes and I start heaving. My legs give way beneath me and I crash to the floor. I wish I had hit my head so that I could sink into a cloudy oblivion, but instead my mind is coming into focus and I wish I could turn away from what it's telling me. It's repeating over and over, like a Buddhist mantra, "It's Barker. Barker is the one who set you up."

CHAPTER TWENTY-SEVEN

When Barker and I got together, I was 44 and she was 28. Two years earlier, I had left Daria, and vowed I'd never get in a long-term relationship again. Daria and I were together for ten years, which was nine years and nine months longer than it should have been. The first three months were blissful. Every other day she showed up with flowers or chocolates or an unexpected gift. She caressed my face, insisting my eyes were the most beautiful she'd ever seen. She made love to me for hours, teasing and tantalizing me in ways that were entirely new to me. I'd never experienced such intensity and passion, and I lapped it up. When she suggested I give up my apartment and move into her house, I had no doubts. But once I moved in, things started changing, although at first I didn't recognize what was happening.

"We're not keeping that futon," she said, directing the mover to take it to the dump.

I loved that lumpy, old mattress, which had been with me since college. "We could put it in the spare room," I suggested.

"I don't need to look at that and be reminded of all the other women you've slept with," she responded. "And anyway, it's mangy-looking." I gave in, and that set the pattern for everything else that happened.

"You need to get a different job," she said, three months after I'd moved in. "Being a preschool teacher doesn't pay you enough to cover half of our expenses."

"I—I thought you said you didn't mind paying the lion's share." Daria worked in real estate and had an endless supply of money.

"Not forever! I'm not going to let a girlfriend mooch off me. Don't you want to be equal partners?"

Even though I loved playing in the sandbox with the kids and reading stories to them, I gave up the funky little preschool job I had and joined Daria in real estate, writing up loans for her potential buyers. The mortgage company was directly connected to Daria's real estate business and customers didn't seem to realize that they weren't always getting the best deal by coming to us. I hated that Daria would make it sound as if they might lose the house if they didn't take one of our loans. I also hated the work itself. I'm hopeless with numbers and even though my part in securing the loans wasn't related to the numbers, it was boring. But the commissions were good and I made four times as much money as I ever had before. It seemed like the perfect time to set up a retirement account, but Daria looked at me as if I were crazy.

"You're thirty years old. You can plan for retirement when you're fifty. We have a lot of living to do, girlfriend!" We bought a boat and spent weekends taking it down the Intracoastal. We threw away our earnings at casinos and spent ridiculous amounts of money on food and alcohol at high-end restaurants. It wasn't the lifestyle I would have chosen, but by then Daria had questioned me about so many of my beliefs and habits that I no longer knew what I wanted.

The gifts stopped the day I moved in to the house, as did most of the compliments. It seemed that now that she had me, Daria wanted me to become someone else.

"You're not really going to wear that hippie jewelry are you?" She'd ask when we were getting dressed to go out and I put on the multitude of silver bangles that I liked to use to cover my arms. When I met her, I was probably wearing ten different bangles and bracelets on each arm and she commented on how unique I was, but that quickly changed to embarrassment at my eccentricity.

The worst part was how she made me doubt myself as a lover. "You don't use your tongue right," she'd scold, as I was snaking my way down her body. "Your fingers are pressing too hard, lighten up!" she'd reprimand as I tried to bring her to orgasm. She stopped teasing and tantalizing me, saying our lovemaking was too one-sided. If I was lucky, I got to have a quick orgasm before it was my turn to go down on her, but after a couple of years even that stopped.

Why did I stay so long? I guess by then, my self-esteem was shot. Instead of praising me outright, as she did at the beginning, she'd give me insults veiled as compliments. *Your face could look fantastic with a nose-job...you could be head of the loan department if you studied accounting in your spare time, instead of making jewelry.* I always felt that if I just tried a little harder, and did everything a little better, our relationship would improve. I did try harder— though thankfully I didn't get the nose-job or give up my jewelry— and it made no difference. I never did get up the courage to leave her though. She left me for a younger woman who was already a rising star in commercial real estate. Three months later, Orlando was blitzed with billboards letting the world know that Daria and Svetlana were the top-selling realtors in town. Their faces were plastered everywhere, Svetlana smiling widely, Daria looking sultry. I couldn't bear to see them, and shortly after, I left the city and moved west to St. Pete.

I met Barker two years later at a fundraiser for the local animal shelter. She approached me and asked if she could sit in one of the unoccupied chairs at the table I was sitting at. I was glad of it, not knowing anyone there. We made easy conversation and at the end of the evening, she asked for my phone number.

"I'm not looking for a date," she said when she saw me hesitate. "I think we could become good friends."

She called a few days later and we met at a coffee shop, where we drank lattes and exchanged stories about our dating histories.

"That's abuse," she said, when I started telling her about Daria.

"Oh no," I reassured her. "She wasn't violent. She never hit me."

"Not with her hands maybe, but she punched you in the gut plenty of times with her words and actions." It was the first time anyone had told me about emotional abuse. The next time we got together, she said, "I hope you don't mind, but I brought you this book to read," and handed me a self-help paperback about psychological cruelty. At first I thought she was overreacting—she was a social worker after all—but then I started opening the book at random places, and every time I did, there was something in it that matched an experience I'd had with Daria. The next time we

155

got together, she gave me another book, this time about how to raise your self-esteem. "I want you to be a strong, confident woman, so that when you're ready to date, you never fall into that trap again."

For the next few weeks, we met a couple of times a week. Gradually, she started introducing me to her social circle. I liked the women I met. They were honest and sincere. None of them boasted about their boats or cars, like the women Daria and I had hung out with, and if they had material wealth, they didn't throw it in your face. What they did talk about was how to improve the world in which they were living and how to support and help each other.

"I choose my friends carefully," she told me when I commented on what I was seeing. "I'd rather have a few intimate friendships with people I know I can trust, than know a boatload of people but not know if they'll be there for me if I really need them."

"What about your family? Can't you rely on them if you need someone?"

"I don't have contact with my family," she responded without elaborating. Later I would learn that she'd grown up surrounded by violence and had decided to create a family of choice instead of interacting with her birth family.

Two months after we met, Barker and I attended a one-woman play about a character who falls in love with another woman despite knowing she has cancer. When it was over, she invited me for herbal tea at her apartment. After she made the tea and we were sitting in her living room, she turned to me and said, "I know you're not looking for a relationship, and nor was I. But I'd really like to date you, if you think you could be interested in me."

I'd had a feeling this was going to come up sooner or later. Although our friendship had blossomed, I'd noticed a certain awkwardness had started to arise between us. At the beginning we'd give each other a quick hug when we met and when we parted, but lately, we'd stopped doing that. For my part, I knew why. Every time she touched me, I felt like a jolt of electricity was shooting through my veins and I wanted to grab her and kiss her. Now it appeared she felt the same way.

"You don't think I'm too old for you?" I said shakily,

knowing that I wanted her to say no. She stood up and took me in her arms. We looked deeply into each other's eyes and then we kissed.

The first time we made love, she asked me what I wanted, what I needed, what I liked.

"I want to make it perfect for you," she told me. "So you'll never want to leave me." Everything about her was the complete opposite of Daria. She didn't shower me with a level of attention she couldn't sustain, she didn't give me backhanded compliments, she didn't try to change me. We waited six months before we moved in together, and when we did, it was to a home that we furnished together. She never made a decision without my input, and she never suggested she knew better than me about anything. She accepted me with all my quirkiness. When I was ditzy or clumsy, she laughed, and when I wore five contrasting necklaces around my neck at the same time, she told me how much she loved my fashion sense. She was the one who suggested I make creating jewelry my full-time occupation, even though it wouldn't bring in enough money to support us.

"Life is too short," she told me. "You can't keep doing work you don't love. My salary is reasonable. It should be enough for us both if we live carefully."

When my mother started to decline, she supported me in every way she could, and when Mom had to move to the nursing home, she cried along with me.

Barker has been my rock for years, and I have never doubted her love for me. I have trusted her with every fiber of my being. So what am I to do now? How should I proceed? The Barker I know would not make me doubt myself or her. The Barker I know would not set me up.

Despite all proof to the contrary, I refuse to believe that I have fallen prey to another woman's abuse. Something must be going on with her, and I have to figure out what.

CHAPTER TWENTY-EIGHT

I dream that Barker is wielding a knife dripping with blood. I dream that Dot and Evie are standing in the background laughing hysterically. I can't figure out what I'm doing and then I realize that Barker has stabbed me and the blood is mine. I try to scream but nothing comes out of my mouth, and then suddenly I'm awake, bathed in sweat. Barker rolls over and spoons me.

"What were you dreaming about? You were groaning terribly."

"I don't remember," I lie. I can still picture the weird grin Barker had on her face as she stood in front of me with the knife.

"Try to relax, my sweetheart," she says sleepily.

"I'm okay." She's already drifting off and I listen as her breathing evens out and she starts snoring quietly.

I strain to remember when the sleepless nights started. I was thinking it had to do with the arrest, but ironically, that was the one night I didn't have bad dreams. It started weeks before that, about the time I started taking Aricept. Since then, that night in jail was the only night I missed a dose. On a whim, I decide to get up and look up the side effects of Aricept. The official website states that side effects are mostly things like nausea and upset stomach but when I study the anecdotal reports from patients, I see that people repeatedly mention interrupted sleep and bad dreams. On the flip side of that, they also mention how much sharper the medication has made them mentally and how much better they can remember things, which makes them willing to put up with the side effects.

I think about my own experience. The areas in which those faceless online people see improvement aren't things I've had difficulty with in the first place. I never got lost, I didn't forget how to drive, I wasn't having difficulty remembering names of friends or family. I've always been a little vague about certain things, like numbers, and I've never been great at holding on to details, but when I picture how my mom was, I really wonder whether I need the Aricept. Of course, I know that those who most need it are the ones who will vehemently deny that they have any memory problems, just like Mom did. But doesn't the fact that I'm aware of this mean that perhaps I really am still of sound mind?

I think back to the day in April when Barker came home from work, bounding through the door, looking more relaxed than she had for a long time. She opened her briefcase and took out a large package of pills. "I got you a trial of Aricept, from Dr. Larson," she said. She didn't need to explain what Aricept was. Mom was on it for years.

"Dr. Larson? Your colleague we visited the other day? How would she have access to medication for dementia? And why would she give you pills for me?"

Barker looked slightly annoyed but then said, "She's not a psychologist, she's a psychiatrist. Don't you remember that I told you she used to work with older adults before she worked with kids? She still has older people in her private practice. She told me that you ought to see an expert for a full workup, but suggested for now you try the medication to see if it would help your memory. Maybe if you take it, you'll remember when I tell you things!" I didn't argue. I knew my memory was hopeless, and if something could help me out, so much the better.

That's what I thought then. But now, reading through the websites and thinking about that whole weird interaction with Dr. Larson, it seems to me that she came to some very quick conclusions without knowing anything about me. I decide to call her first thing in the morning. Meanwhile I do a little more research on what steps go into making a diagnosis of dementia.

***

Dr. Larson says she will be happy to meet me at her home

159

office this evening. I ask her not to mention the appointment to Barker and she assures me she won't.

I drive over to her home and make my way to her office. After I climb the curved steps, inlaid with the colorful Mexican tile that I remember discussing with her, she ushers me into her office. I realize that this is the same room we sat in last time, not a private living room. I think back to that visit and how weird I thought she was, but if we were in her office and she thought I was there as a patient, then I probably made a similar impression on her.

As soon as we're seated, I ask her, "When I came to see you last time, were you under the impression that I was here for an evaluation?"

"Certainly I was." She looks askance, as if wondering what other reason we had for being there. I'm pretty sure Barker told me it had something to do with her work and I wonder whether she purposely misled me, or whether I wasn't paying enough attention to what she said. We met with a couple of her colleagues socially that same week. Perhaps she really did tell me Dr. Larson was going to evaluate me.

"I thought we were paying you a social visit. As a result, I think you may have come up with some very false conclusions about me. In fact, I'd like you to do a formal evaluation now. Because I'm pretty sure I don't have anything beyond menopausal fog combined with a few senior moments." Dr. Larson sighs and I realize that she is so used to her dementia patients denying their diagnosis that I am not helping myself. "But, if you tell me that I have serious impairments, I will believe you one hundred percent. Does that sound fair?" She looks relieved and nods her head.

She begins by asking me where we are and who she is. She moves on to ask me who the current President is (I tell her) and which famous actor was President in the 1980s ("the one who had Alzheimer's?" I ask with a twinkle in my eye, "Reagan."). Then she asks me to remember three words which she will repeat later.

"Shirt. Brown. Honesty." I'm a little surprised by the words. When I looked up the test online, it suggested they would be a little more commonplace, like apple and horse. But I'm determined to ace this part of the test and I immediately start to make word associations in my mind. I tell myself that Dr. Larson is wearing a brown shirt and that if I'm honest, I don't like it. I repeat the words to myself as she continues with her next question. She asks me how the words arm and leg are comparable and I assure her that they are parts of the body. She asks me to spell "world" backward, which I do, and then asks me to count back from 100 to 50 in series of seven. I tell her that math isn't my strongest suit, but still I stumble from 100 to 93 to 86 and so on until she stops me. She asks me what it means if someone tells me not to put all my eggs in one basket. I'm tempted to make a joke and tell her that knowing me, it would be because the basket is likely on the front of my bike and when I ride over a speed bump they'll all crack; but instead I tell her as calmly as I can that it means it's important to diversify, whether it's money or hopes. I can see she's impressed by that answer. She jots something down, then looks up and says, "What were the three words I asked you to remember?" For a moment my heart beats wildly and my mind goes blank. Horse? Apple? No, I made up a sentence: it had to do with her... "I honestly don't like your brown shirt," I blurt out and she smiles as I correct myself. "Shirt, Brown, Honesty."

She asks me to draw a clock face and make the clock point to ten to three and I wonder how future generations will do this task, since I suspect most of them think of a timepiece as a square digital device, whether on the wall or their wrist. I'm tempted to draw something ornate and unusual—a round clock face is so boring—but I remind myself why she's asked me to do this task, and force myself to draw a simple circle with long and short hands inside it, pointing to the appropriate places. She asks me to take a piece of paper and fold it a certain way and I comply.

At the end of the test, she frowns and my heart sinks. What did I do wrong? Surely I answered everything correctly. I wait for her to say something, but she looks down at her pad.

"How did I do?" I ask, not able to wait any longer.

She looks up. "You did fine. Better than fine. You scored a perfect 30 out of 30."

"Fantastic!" I heave an enormous sigh of relief.

"But you're still on Aricept, so really there are two possibilities. Either you don't have any form of dementia, or the Aricept is working perfectly. The only way to know which, is for you to stop taking the medication and for me to repeat the test next week, once the drug has exited your system. I'm willing to do that if you are."

I assure her that I'm more than willing and we agree to meet the same time next week. Before I leave, I have another question for her.

"If someone is depressed, could it make them do things that are completely out of character?" I ask.

"Do you feel depressed?" A look of concern comes over her. "Because sometimes the symptoms of dementia mask depression."

"No, not me. B—" I stop myself. I don't want to put Barker in any kind of awkward position at work. "But a friend I know might be. She doesn't come across as sad or droopy, but she's done a couple of things lately that I think are kinda off the wall."

"It's definitely possible. There are various types of depression, and one type is called depression with psychosis. It can be almost like having schizophrenia—people can have delusions or hallucinations, and get completely misdiagnosed."

"Thanks," I say, and mean it. This may just explain a whole lot more than I expected.

***

The next piece of research I need to do is to find out more about Mrs. Clark. Front and center, I need to find the twin daughters who will have nothing to do with her. As soon as Barker leaves for work the next morning I go back on the computer and try to locate the blog her daughter wrote. If only I could remember the daughter's name, but I didn't write it down and my mind's a complete blank. I try to remember how I found it. I know I was looking up Ava and somehow stumbled upon that blog entry. I waste an hour trying every different way I can think of, and in despair, I type in 'why I don't speak to my mom' and lo and behold, up comes a blog by April Clark. Yes! Now I have to figure out how I can interact with her. I click on the icon asking me if I'd like to subscribe to her blog, then scroll through other entries she's written to see what else she may have said about her mother. But she never mentions her. Most of the entries are about living a life full of integrity. I go back to the one she wrote about her mom and reply to it, telling her that the post was very inspiring, and asking if we can talk about it in person.

"Who are you?" She writes back, and I realize that from her perspective I could be any kind of whacko and that it would make sense that she wouldn't talk to a total stranger. I ask if I can private message her. "Only if you tell me who you are. Can I look you up on Facebook or LinkedIn?" Naturally, I do not have accounts on either of these sites. I decide I will have to be honest with her.

"I think your mom is getting me into trouble," I write, hoping like heck that she won't block me from the blog. No response. I go up to my studio and create a complicated necklace with amber and wire and then come back down to the computer. Still nothing. I must have blown it. Why was I so impatient? I could have been a little less blunt. But that's me, I always barge into things without thinking. I wonder how I can find her sister Astrid to see if I could get any information from her instead. I Google her name but nothing comes up, not even a suggestion to look her up on Facebook. Damn. I need to know what happened with those daughters. An idea is forming in my mind, but knowing about Mrs. Clark's past is essential. I go back upstairs and spend the rest of the afternoon creating a pendant with a gorgeous piece of olive-green Moldovite I found last year and have been waiting to use. I've read that it opens up the heart chakra and as I hold its jagged edges in my hand, I can almost feel the vibrations pulsing through me. I decide to set it in an asymmetric sterling silver base. I become so absorbed in what I'm doing, that I'm oblivious to the front door banging when Barker comes home. I'm only aware of her presence when she pushes open the door to my craft room and says, "Who is April Clark? And why are you trying to contact her?"

CHAPTER TWENTY-NINE

My hand squeezes the Moldovite and I remind myself that it opens up the heart. This is what I need right now. To approach Barker with serenity and love.

"Why are you trying to contact April Clark?" she demands again. "What's going on?"

"I'm pretty sure April is Ava Clark's estranged daughter. I want to find out why they don't talk to each other."

"But why? What business is it of yours? Do you still think Mrs. Clark set you up?"

My heart starts to hammer. I have to think quickly. How should I respond to this?

"No," I reply calmly. "I don't."

Barker comes in and clears a space off the other stool in my studio so that she can sit down. "Then why would you want to know about her relationship with her daughter?"

"Because I need to know whether or not she's an appropriate foster parent for the girls."

Barker's expression turns to one of disbelief. "I can't believe you. That has nothing to do with you. Why don't you focus on what's going on with your own stuff?"

"It has everything to do with me."

She looks at me like I've gone completely mad. I lean across the table and take her hand.

"Sweetheart," I speak very slowly, and distinctly. "I know what you did and I think I know why you did it."

Her face pales. "What are you talking about?"

"I know you set me up. No—don't deny it. I've spoken to Parminder."

She pulls her hand away from mine. "What? How…?"

"I also know you don't hate me and that everything you've done, could only have been in my best interests." I take her hand again and hold it firmly in mine. She lowers her face, her chin disappearing into her neck. I pull it up gently, and look into her eyes. I will not be afraid. I know what is there. "I love you Barker, and I know you love me. And I also know you framed me."

Barker's pupils grow big within her blue eyes as her expression changes from fear, to love, to shame. I see it all, the emotions that she has bottled up for so many months. Suddenly her whole body starts heaving and she bursts into loud, wailing sobs, the tears pouring down her face. She folds her arms on the table and buries her head within them.

"What have I done?" She looks up for a moment and whispers, "What have I done?"

I get up from where I'm sitting and kneel on the floor next to her. I lift her face gently and cup it in my hands. "Nothing that we can't solve together, my love, nothing that we can't work out."

***

Downstairs, we head back to the computer. April has responded to my request. It was the pop-up on the screen that caught Barker's eye before she came upstairs to find me. April has agreed to email me. A rapid-fire back and forth of emails quickly nets me the information I've been looking for. Mr. Clark was a mean-spirited bully. April doesn't know whether her mom didn't mention the bats earlier on purpose, or whether she truly didn't think of it until it was too late.

Did she love him? I ask. *Was she sorry he died?*

Hard to know. She always stood up for him, always took his side.

His side?

Yeah. I told her Dad did something inappropriate to me when I was younger and she told me I must have imagined it, that perhaps I was too young to understand what his true intent was. I said I knew exactly what his intent was. She just kept saying, "I know he can be a bit of a tough nut sometimes, but he loves you girls, he always wants the best for you." I couldn't get through

165

to her, so I stopped trying and decided to just cut off the connection altogether.

Did you ever report him?

No, it was so long ago, and I had no proof.

Did you know that your parents had become foster parents?

What? No! Oh, please don't tell me—

No, nothing as far as we know. It sounds like your mom never did anything to you girls, though, right?

No. Although not believing me is a form of abuse in my mind. But I wouldn't ever want to see her parent another child. If she didn't stand up for her own birth children, how would she ever stand up for her foster kids? What if she gets involved with some other guy and the same thing happens?

Barker is watching as we type back and forth. I have found out what I need to know and I end the conversation.

***

Next, we head into the kitchen. "I'm going to make us some peppermint tea and we're going to talk," I tell her. Barker's always the one in charge, but today it is my turn. She nods and follows me, seating herself at the kitchen counter, watching as I put the kettle on the stove. I think about what I want to know first and I realize it's not the part about me.

"Why the girls?" I ask gently. "Why Kallie and Michaela?" Why would she send two harmless foster children into a potentially dangerous situation? It's so out of keeping with who she is.

"I guess I just snapped. I got so sick and tired of all these foster parents cleaning up after people who just don't seem to get what they're doing to their kids. I wanted to shock Kallie and Mikki's birth moms into caring enough to do the right thing. I thought if they saw a visual of how their daughters could end up, they'd agree to give up their parental rights so Mrs. Clark could adopt them both."

The water boils and I pour it into our mugs as I ponder what she's saying. What I realize is that she is burned out, completely burned out. Over the years, we've talked about how social workers deal with all the horrors and tragedies, day in and day out. She's told me stories about colleagues leaving the profession and taking their lives in a totally different direction because they can't face the sordidness of their work. She's told me about some of the more hopeless situations that can never have a happy ending. But I always thought she was taking care of herself. We tried to do all the right things for her. We traveled to exotic countries, took plenty of fun vacations, did everything we could to ensure she was leading a balanced life, but somewhere along the line it's caught up with her.

"I know you, Barker, I know you wouldn't want to harm those girls."

"Are you kidding? That's the last thing I would ever do. I've known them for ten years. In a way, I love them. That's why I wanted to make everything right for them. Mrs. Clark was such a good foster mother. I'd never seen them so happy as they've been in that home. But their moms were never going to let them go so I had to force the situation. And it almost worked. It would have, if things hadn't started to go wrong." I'm so struck by the irony of what's happening. Everyone thinks I'm the one who might be going crazy, but it turns out Barker's already there. Although her words make sense, the sentiments behind them don't. How could anyone, let alone a social worker, think what she did could have been justified?

"Tell me everything," I say, "how you set the whole thing up." I see the relief in her eyes. Her shoulders suddenly relax and I realize that it's exactly what she wants and needs to do.

"I had to plan everything so carefully," she says, and I can hear a tone of pride in her voice. "It all had to happen while I was out of town. I had to time it so Parminder would play her part, but then leave right away. Months ago we'd started talking about what she'd do with her summer. Once I'd decided on my plan, I told her about the program in Guatemala and helped set it up for her. I timed going to the retreat so that my first day there would be the day after she left the agency. On her last day, when she was packing up, I told her to keep her county badge as a souvenir. It was deactivated so I knew she couldn't use it, but to an outsider it still looked official. Then I called her two hours before she was due to leave for the airport and told her I needed a favor."

"What if she'd had someone there with her or if she'd said no?" I ask.

"She'd already told me she was getting a taxi to the airport. I knew she wasn't the type to still be packing last-minute. I figured she'd have her suitcase already sitting by her front door, and be playing video games or something."

"So the favor was asking her to get the girls. What reason did you give?" Neither of us has touched our tea. We sit across from each other at the kitchen table, having the strangest conversation I've ever had.

"I told her we got a child abuse report on the hotline about Mrs. Clark. She'd never met the Clarks or Kallie or Michaela. I said I was sure it was nothing but that it had to be checked out."

I am struck by the irony of this. Barker was so sure Mrs. Clark's home was perfect, but after my email exchange with April, we know better now.

I take a guess at the next part. "You told her they were eighteen and that you'd arranged for them to go to a fancy condo while the investigation took place." She nods. "Didn't that strike her as odd?"

"She didn't have time to think about it. I said it had to be done right away. I knew she was more focused on getting her plane than on listening to a whole lot of details."

"What if she'd just said no?"

"I knew she wouldn't. Removing children from a home was one thing she still hadn't done. I was pretty sure she'd want to rise to the challenge when I explained that these girls were going to be really upset, especially since we obviously couldn't tell them the reason they were being removed."

"But afterward, anyone could have emailed her and asked her about it. How did you know she wouldn't be checking email?"

She shakes her head and raises her eyebrows.

"Honestly, Wynn, it was exhausting doing all the planning. I had to think of every little detail. I knew her work email would be disabled the day she left but I had to do something about her personal email. So I set up a bunch of fake email accounts and started spamming her like crazy. At first she blocked the emails, so then I got more personal so it would freak her out. Finally, she closed the email account."

"Didn't you feel bad, doing all that?"

I watch Barker closely. It's almost as if I'm in the room with someone I don't know. Barker is here physically but she's not present. Her face barely registers any emotion as she describes everything to me.

She nods. "Of course I felt bad. But social workers have to

do things that feel bad all the time. Parminder's strong and she's smart. I knew this would be just a blip for her. Anyway, I didn't feel completely terrible because right up until the end, she was still acting like a know-it-all."

"What do you mean?"

"On that final phone call, I was all magnanimous. Told her I'd enjoyed working with her and even apologized for times when I might have been brusque. You know what she said?" Obviously I don't, and she plows on. "Oh, that's okay Ms. Barker. I never took anything personally. You're a lot older than me and I think you're jaded. It's natural. You've been in the business for so long."

It appears Parminder had Barker figured out a long time before I did. Too bad the student didn't realize quite how burned out Barker really is.

"Whose was the condo in Pelican Beach?" I ask.

"Some guy who lives up north. I saw the ad in the Gazette and rented it for a month."

"And then what?"

"I figured the girls would just be there for a couple of days. I bought real nice food for them and stocked the fridge and pantry with all their favorites. Oh and I got beer and joints in for Damon as well."

"Who's Damon?"

"I needed photos of the girls in compromising situations. Damon was the one I picked to do that."

"Barker!" For the first time, I'm really shocked. She set those girls up with some guy and isn't even ashamed of it?

"No, wait, it's not what you think. I didn't tell him I wanted the pictures to look suggestive. I told him they were foster kids aging out and that I'd arranged for a special kind of treat for them before real life hit. I said he should have a party with them, give them a good time, and that I wanted to surprise them with blow-up photos of them modeling. I told him to take the photos with the girls' phones and that I'd give the girls back their devices when I picked them up the next day. These kids are streetwise. I knew they might have some of the beer and maybe even smoke a joint or two but Kallie knows how to take care of herself, and she's very protective of Mikki."

"But what if he'd raped them?"

Barker shakes her head and looks at me, her eyes wide, as if she can't understand how I could even imagine she'd put the girls in that kind of danger.

"Damon's a good guy. Stupid, but not evil."

"How do you know? Who is he?" So many thoughts are swirling through my brain I can't keep them all in order. But I need to try to hear everything and keep my mind clear.

"A client I used to have in Family Preservation. He's trying to get his son back but keeps failing. He's one of those who mean well, but the system's rigged against him. He has to take mandated classes, but they're always at times when he's working. He can't take time off work because he's scared he'd lose his job, and he has to have a job to prove he can keep a roof over his kid's head I told him if he did something for me, I'd do something for him."

"But you don't know what a guy would do in a situation like that."

"I knew he might want to mess around with them a bit, but that he'd never do anything they wouldn't agree to."

"But they're fifteen…"

"Weren't you frisky at fifteen? You know you were, and so was I, and so are they. We don't have to kid ourselves about that."

I know she's trying to rationalize her crazy, awful behavior, but what she says is true. When I was growing up, we thought it was a badge of honor if an older guy was interested in us. When I was sixteen I had a twenty-two-year-old boyfriend and thought I was the coolest thing around. He would show up on my doorstep in a tailored white suit, looking every bit like a Greek John Travolta and Mom would welcome him in with her standard pot of tea and ginger biscuits, before sending us off dancing. I was proud of the fact that somebody so mature took me seriously. But things are different these days and Barker knows it. Does she really believe what she's telling me?

"So they ended up being by themselves, with no phones or any way to communicate with anyone for over a week?"

"It wasn't meant to go on for nearly that long!" Barker looks genuinely upset about this, twisting the ring on her finger round and round in agitation. "I had no idea Mrs. Clark would leave on a trip. I thought I'd go to her house and she'd be there and I could get the investigation started. But instead she wasn't there and I had to wait until she got back. And then everything else got delayed. The pictures were meant to arrive the next day. Mikki's mom had been at the same place for months so I thought she'd see them right away. I had no idea she'd been kicked out a week earlier. I did know it might take a couple of days for Kallie's mom to get her photos in prison, but I thought as soon as the officer screening the mail saw that letter, she'd alert someone. I didn't know that stupid prison guard would put the letter aside instead of showing it to someone straight away."

She's been talking nonstop, almost in a trance. Suddenly she looks up at me. "Oh my god, Wynn, that part was awful. I stocked the condo pretty well but I didn't want the girls to run out of food. I knew they must be getting pretty bored and upset the longer they were there. I was desperate to get them out, but I had to wait for it all to fall into place."

"And meanwhile, you acted as if you knew nothing? You told me how worried you were about the girls, when all the time you knew where they were."

"The moment Parminder put the plan in motion, I knew I had to start acting as if I had no idea about anything that had happened. I had to imagine exactly how I would have felt and behaved if I really had no idea what was going on. I did it with you and I did it when I went to see Mrs. Clark. I knew before I set the ball rolling that if I didn't come across as worried, or surprised, I might slip up in some other way. But it was the weirdest thing because the more I did it, the more I just fell into believing the role I was playing. Part of me really was scared that she'd taken them out of state, and I felt genuinely surprised when she said someone had taken them. I know you think I was acting with you, but in a way, I really wasn't."

I need to do something so I pick up our cups, no longer steaming but still full of tea, and throw the liquid in the sink. I think about what she said and whether it's possible to get to a point where you believe your own lies. It could be part of the depression I think she's suffering from. Or what she said could be possible. It happened to me once. Daria was so jealous that sometimes I'd make up something to appease her, and then forget I made it up. Once when a work colleague gave me an expensive perfume she couldn't wear because of allergies, I told Daria I bought it myself on a whim. The following week when my colleague commented on the perfume, I told her I'd treated myself to it. "It's not the one I gave you?" she asked, and I realized what I'd done. So I sort of understand what Barker's saying. But there's still so much more I don't understand.

"I get that you were sick and tired of birth moms not having to answer for their shortcomings. I get that at some point you got so burned out that you just snapped. But why not just leave your job? Why hang in there if you were so done with it? And why work so hard to become a supervisor, when that would have been just as bad, if not worse, than what you do now?"

"Because we couldn't afford for me to leave my job. Not with you doing your jewelry."

"But why not ask me to give up my jewelry? Surely you know I wouldn't want you to be miserable at work?"

"But that's the weird part. I'm not miserable. Not all the time anyway. There are parts of my job that I love. I care about the kids and I want them to have good homes. Even in the middle of this whole mess, when Parminder told me she thought I was burned out, I was shocked."

There is still another piece, the one I dread asking her about. But I'm too wiped out. It will wait until tomorrow.

Slowly we climb the stairs to our bedroom. As we get into bed, Barker turns toward me and takes my hands in hers.

"Wynn, I…" tears are falling down her cheeks.

"I know you do. I love you too."

"But I—"

"I know you didn't."

"There's more I need to tell you."

"Tomorrow." I'm so tired I can't keep my eyes open. Tonight I'm going to sleep the sleep of the dead.

CHAPTER THIRTY

I sleep solidly until ten in the morning, and it's not because I've stopped taking the Aricept. It's because I know that whatever's going to happen from here on, I'll be okay. I open my eyes and stretch out. Barker's side of the bed is empty, which doesn't surprise me, as she never sleeps past eight, even on a weekend or holiday. I suspect also, that she may not have slept as well as I did. For the first time in a very long time, I feel grounded and secure which is ironic, given that I discovered that my girlfriend had set me up as a suspect in a crime and also made me appear like a demented loony. But it's all over now, or at least, it's almost all over. We have some intense talking to do but I know that Barker will do the right thing.

I pull myself out of bed, aware that the long hours lying down have exacerbated my arthritis, and stumble to the bathroom. As I brush my teeth and catch sight of my reflection in the mirror, I can see that something in my demeanor has changed. All those years with Daria took their toll, but when I moved in with Barker, I thought I was done with the mousy, insecure person I'd been. I see now that I wasn't. Today is the first day I can look at myself and see a wise, even beautiful, older woman. As I try to bring order to my unruly tresses, I notice that somewhere along the line, my hair has transformed from the mealy oatmeal color it was, to a beautiful silver. As I look at my eyes, I see new lines around them, but they are lines etched from maturity, not age. Now I must use that maturity to deal with the one topic I avoided yesterday.

In the kitchen, Barker has laid out a delicious breakfast of granola and strawberries with fresh croissants that she must have bought this morning. From the lack of barking, I surmise that Barker is out with the dogs. She walks in just as I am pouring almond milk onto my granola. Queen and Latifah jump all over me and I tousle their fur before standing up to give Barker a hug. I chop up the strawberries and she goes to the fridge to pour herself a glass of juice. I know she's waiting for me to say something, and I also know I can't make small talk.

"I could ask you questions, tease it all out of you, but why don't you just tell me why you set me up." Earlier, I thought about how I wanted to hear it, and what I wanted to hear, and I realized that it would only make sense if I got the whole story at once. "When did it start?"

"Months ago." She brings her juice to the counter and sits on a stool. "Or perhaps years ago, when I watched your mom decline. I remember the early signs that we both ignored. We used to laugh at how disorganized she was and make jokes about her hopeless memory. After she was diagnosed and got so bad, I told myself I wouldn't let that happen with you. Women whose moms have Alzheimer's have a higher risk of getting it themselves and I had no idea that you weren't genetically related. I became extra vigilant, and the more I watched, the more I saw. You kept forgetting things, you'd muddle up times, space out when I gave you information, and then swear I never told you."

"But that's nothing new! I've been doing that for years."

"I know. You've always been ditzy. Everyone always calls you the absent-minded professor or asks whether you have attention deficit disorder. But for me, it felt like it was getting worse. That time we went to Pelican Bay and you said you didn't remember ever being there, that was scary. When I'd come home from work and find you'd forgotten to walk the dogs, I got nervous. I even asked Dot and Evie to keep an eye out and see what they thought. And once I did that, it was like we all noticed more things, like that time you came to the wrong restaurant."

"And the following week? Did I really get the time wrong, or were you trying to prove a point to Dot an Evie?"

"I—I may have told you the wrong time. But then when I saw you, your pants were stained and you had on winter shoes even though it was a hot summer's day. All I could think of was how your mom started to get confused with her clothes and not know how to dress appropriately."

"But didn't you notice all the times that I did dress properly? And that I did get to the right place at the right time?"

"No, I suppose I didn't. I was too focused on looking for mistakes. Like when you put the wrong initials on Dot's necklace, I felt terrible. I still wasn't completely convinced, but then when we went to see Dr. Larson and you acted so weird, that's when I knew I had to do something. You were clearly going downhill."

"But I'm sure you told me we were paying a social visit!"

"Honestly, sweetheart, I didn't. I think when you're really focused on your jewelry and are busy making up some design in your head, you just don't pay attention to what I'm saying. We socialized with a couple of people when I thought I had a chance to get a promotion, but I told you exactly who Dr. Larson was and why we were going to see her."

I break off a piece of croissant absent-mindedly, and then think about all the other things I do without really paying any attention.

"Do you still think I'm in the early stages of Alzheimer's?"

"I'm not sure. Do you think so?"

"No. When you suggested I take medication for my memory, I thought it might be a good idea, and maybe it still is. But that's all it would be for—to help my memory. I don't have any difficulty with cognitive processing, and I don't have any serious deficits. The other day I went back to Dr. Larson—"

"You did? She never said anything."

"No, because I asked her not to. I scored perfectly on the mental status exam. She admitted that it might be because I was on Aricept and we agreed that I should stop taking it and she'll re-test me. But I'm pretty sure that even if I score 28 instead of 30, I'm fine. You just have to accept, as you always have, that sometimes I don't pay attention, sometimes I'm distracted, and sometimes I just don't remember things."

Barker sighs. It's been the one area in our relationship where we've had disagreements. She has a hard time believing that even when I try, I just can't hold onto information. She can't believe that I don't notice things that need doing around the house and need to have them pointed out to me. She thinks everyone is like her, detail-oriented and fully engaged in their surroundings.

"I'll try," she says.

I look at the clock. We're meant to be joining Dot and Evie for a tour of one of the local historic mansions, but we aren't done yet. Now I must turn to the more difficult question.

"Assuming that you thought I had Alzheimer's, I'm still not sure I understand why you would set me up as the villain in your foster-kid scheme." It comes out a little harsher than I mean it to, but I can't help it. Even though I trust Barker, I still have a hard time believing she put me through this.

"It was the finances. We used up everything to keep your mom in that nursing home. I kept going over in my mind what would happen to you when your condition deteriorated, which it seemed to be doing. I knew that I couldn't give up my job to stay home and look after you because we'd have nothing to live on. I had to keep working. But as long as we had my salary, I knew you wouldn't be eligible for state help. So I couldn't see how I could make it work: I wouldn't be able to afford to look after you, but I also couldn't afford to put you in a facility."

She's been standing by the window this entire time, but now she comes over to me. "I started having all those thoughts about Kallie's mom and how mad I was at her for pretty much ruining Kallie's life. I wanted to get back at her, and all the other moms, but I couldn't figure out how to go about it without putting suspicion on someone other than myself. Then I realized that if you got charged with a crime, and you were already on Aricept and had a diagnosis, instead of taking you to prison, they'd put you in a locked facility, which is where you'd need to be anyway once the Alzheimer's got really bad."

"Barker, I— "

"No, listen. Because of my past jobs, I know the facilities they use for people in that situation. There's a really good one locally, nicer even than some of the nursing homes where paying clients end up. So I thought it would be the perfect solution: you'd be well cared for, I could use money from my salary to bring you anything you needed, and I'd be able to see you as often as possible."

I get up and pile my dishes and mug into the sink. I think about her explanation. I pay attention to every word, every nuance.

What she did was wrong and terrible, yet all I can hear is love and concern. "Nonetheless, it was crazy," I think, and then realize I've said it out loud.

"Why didn't you talk to Dot and Evie about it? Why keep all the crazy thoughts inside so that they warped your whole thought process?"

"I figured if I told them, they'd offer to pay for whatever we needed. It's one thing to let them pay for dinner, quite another to pay for a top-quality nursing home."

"That's what friends are for. I'm not sure they would have offered that much, but if they did, it would be because they wanted to support you, support us both."

"I guess it's just me, trying too hard to be independent."

I nod in agreement. "So what happens now? You're going to get me out of this fix I'm in, right?" I ask.

"Yes," she says. "Somehow we can get this worked out."

"What's to work out? You'll have to go to Detective Gordon and tell him the truth." She falls silent. "Right? I'm sure they'll take it easy on you, with your background."

"Maybe." She doesn't sound convinced. "I guess so."

"When I talked to Dr. Larson, I asked her whether depression could make people do things that are out of character. She said it can do all kinds of crazy things to a person. I think you're depressed, and I bet she would agree. That would make for mitigating circumstances. I'm sure between that and everything you've done throughout your career, you could get some kind of plea agreement."

She puts her head down, deep in thought, then looks up. "I'll have to do it. What I'd like to do is cancel with Dot and Evie and enjoy the rest of the day with you today. Tomorrow I'll go back to the retreat center for a day to get myself truly centered and calm, and then Monday, I'll turn myself in. How does that sound?"

To show my agreement, I unbutton her shirt. Then I lead her back upstairs and for the first time in a long time, we make love, tenderly and fiercely, as if it were the first time and the last time, all rolled into one.

CHAPTER THIRTY-ONE

Barker leaves for the retreat center early, while I'm still asleep. I wake up and luxuriate in having the whole bed to myself, planning my day. At first, I think I will spend it crafting jewelry for the competition, but then I decide instead to try something new. I asked Barker to be patient with my ditzy ways, but the other side of that is that I have to start making an effort to pay more attention. So today, I will start to focus on all the small things that need to be done, and attend to all the details I usually miss. I will clean the house and give the dogs the attention they deserve. I will make Barker's favorite lasagna for dinner. And if I have time, only then, will I do my jewelry.

I am so proud of Barker for owning up and doing the right thing. If she goes to Gordon first thing tomorrow morning, then I don't think they'll keep her overnight at central booking. (How easily that term rolls off my tongue. A month ago, I wouldn't even have known what it was.) How will he react to her confession? I have a moment of panic when I think that he might suspect she's just doing it to protect me and won't believe her, but then I remember that she'll be able to give him so much proof, it will be irrefutable. I'm pretty sure that because of all the work she's done for the community, and all the people she knows in law enforcement, they'll be able to give her a pretty good plea bargain.

The thing that probably won't happen is what I'd been hoping for before I knew what Barker had done. I thought Barker and I should adopt Kallie and Michaela. Once I found out that Mrs. Clark had issues with her own daughters, Barker adopting Kallie and Michaela seemed like an obvious choice. The girls adore

Barker, and she cares so much about them. But I'm still struggling to reconcile that with the fact that she put them in harm's way. I guess we'll just have to wait and see how it all turns out.

I spend the day in a whirlwind of activity and by early evening, the house is spotless, the dogs are fed, and dinner is bubbling in the oven. I call Barker's cell phone to see if she's on her way home yet, but it goes directly to her voicemail. I take the lasagna out of the oven and decide to go up to my studio and work on some jewelry until she gets home. I quickly become absorbed in a complicated bracelet design and by the time I check my watch, it's three hours later. I start to get nervous. I call Barker's cell phone and again it goes to voicemail. I take the dogs for their last walk of the day and then I decide I'm going to call the retreat center. I root around for the emergency number she left me the last time she went, and dial it. *Please let someone answer*, I pray silently.

My entreaty is answered when a voice comes on the line.

"Namaste. How may I help you?"

"I'm sorry to bother you so late," I say, "but could you tell me if my partner, Barker, is still there?"

"Is that a first name or last name?"

"It's both. She just goes by Barker."

"Which program is she with?"

"No program. She just came up for the day."

"We don't have any day programs. All our retreats are at least two nights."

"It was a last-minute thing. She just wanted to clear her head. Could you just see whether she left already?" There is silence, except for the rustling of some papers.

"I'm sorry, but there's no record she was here today."

I feel my heart start to sink, but I can't give up yet.

"Is there a chance that she was there without registering?"

"No. Everyone has to sign in at the gate. If she'd come here today, her name would be on the list."

I hang up and feel all the goodwill and positive energy I've had today drain out of me entirely.

She has run away. She had no intention of turning herself in. She has chosen the coward's way out.

***

179

The next morning, when there is still no sign of Barker, and no message, I call Detective Gordon and ask if I can meet with him. Without giving him any details, I tell him that Barker and I had a long talk and she implicated herself in the kidnapping and abduction.

"You understand I'm having a hard time believing this. I've worked with Barker for fifteen years. I think I know her pretty well." He looks at me skeptically.

"And I've loved her for seventeen years and thought the same thing. I could tell you more but that would be wasting time. Barker's disappeared. She's gone, and I need your help finding her."

"It makes no sense. How do I know you're not making this up? Worse—how do I know you haven't done something to her?"

"You don't. That's why we need to find her. You're a detective—you can locate her car, check her phone records. I can't do any of that. You can also contact Parminder to corroborate the first part of my story." I give him the information about the Peace Project and he says he'll make some calls.

I go home, but I can't settle down. I pace the house, making the dogs nervous. Having swept and vacuumed yesterday, the only thing I can think to do is to clean the oven and the fridge. When the phone rings, I jump nervously, wanting an answer, and dreading one.

"We located her car in the airport parking lot." My heart plummets to new depths. She has fled. Instead of confessing, she has chosen to leave me and the dogs and run away. But where would she go? She has no family she can turn to. Then he gives me more information. "We ran her credit card, but didn't find any purchase of a ticket. However, the FAA confirmed that she used her passport and we tracked down her name on a flight to Guatemala. We checked the car rental agencies and found one in which an American rented a car for a day, but never brought it back."

"Was it Barker?"

"The car was booked under the name of Rosalind Larimer, which was also the name on the credit card used to pay for her flight. What am I to make of the fact that Larimer is your last name?"

"Rosalind was my mother," I whisper. My head feels thick as if it's stuffed with cotton balls. "She died two years ago." Detective Gordon says nothing and I can't tell what he's thinking. "Did Barker go to Parminder at the Peace Project?"

"We don't know. But here's the strange part. Parminder left the Project suddenly yesterday. Nobody saw her go, and the note she left didn't give any clue as to where she was headed."

Then he tells me that Barker has booked a flight home for today but she wasn't on it. Despite the fact that she missed the flight, my heart lifts slightly. She booked a return flight! She's not leaving me. I don't know why she went to Guatemala but she's obviously trying to sort something out with Parminder. It doesn't make sense because when she confessed to me, she didn't implicate Parminder. She said she just used her to get the girls into the condo.

"She must be trying to persuade Parminder to come back with her," I say.

There's a silence on the other end of the phone.

"We're concerned that there's been some sort of accident, or foul play. Shortly after Barker arrived in Guatemala and Parminder left the Peace Project a monsoon hit that area. If they were out in it, there's no telling what might have happened to them."

And that's when I know something bad has happened, something really bad.

***

Late the following day, Detective Gordon stops by the house.

"The Guatemalan authorities found the abandoned rental car not that far from the Peace Project. Barker's passport was inside the car."

I walk slowly down the hall, into the kitchen. I sit at the table and put my head down, trying to swallow the sob that is starting to rise in my throat.

Detective Gordon follows me.

"Wynn, when you first came to me to tell me Barker had

disappeared, you said Barker had implicated herself in all of this when she talked to you. Why did you tell me that?"

"What do you mean?" I raise my head and look at him. I see confusion, but also compassion in his tired eyes.

"Inside the car, they found a confession written by Parminder."

"They—what? *Parminder* confessed...?" It makes no sense. My mind is whirling.

"Yes. It's the same lettering that was used in the letter that was sent to Kallie and Michaela's birth parents. She must have had it ready all along. Our best guess is that Barker must have figured out it was Parminder who set up the kidnapping, and she wanted to get her to return to the USA."

"So where are they now?"

"As we knew, the local authorities said that the afternoon Parminder left the Peace Project it started raining torrentially. It didn't stop until today. They think if Parminder and Wynn went into the jungle where the car was parked, there's not much hope they could have made it out."

I feel as if he's stabbing me with sharp knives with every sentence. I can barely bring myself to voice my next question. "Have they searched for...for...?" I can't say the word. It is too final.

"Bodies? They said hopefully they can start tomorrow, when the flooding has subsided a little more."

I feel my chest heave and my throat catch. Suddenly sobs are wracking my body. The detective gets up and puts his hand awkwardly on my shoulder.

"If it's any consolation, I think Barker may have been a hero. She must have realized Parminder set up the whole thing and she was trying to make it right by going there in person. She didn't want you to know, until she'd sorted it out. You know Barker. She's a problem solver."

He uses the present tense, but I know I will never see her again. I also know he's wrong about Parminder. It wasn't her. I have a sick feeling in my stomach, because I think Barker decided to pin it all on Parminder. I'm about to tell Detective Gordon that, and then I think, what's the point? Everyone knows Barker was a wonderful, hard-working social worker and a loving partner. Why should I discredit her name if I don't need to?

***

Two days later, Detective Gordon comes to the house again, this time with a young female cop. I think it's the same one who arrested me, but I'm in such a fog, I can't keep anything straight at the moment.

I know why they've come and I don't want to hear what they have to say.

"Can I get you something to drink?" I offer, stalling the inevitable. Mom always said a cup of tea solves every problem, but this is one time I don't think she's right.

They shake their heads. The young female takes my arm and guides me to the sofa. She sits me down and goes to the kitchen.

"Their bodies have been found," Detective Gordon says, as the young cop approaches me with a glass of water. "I'm sorry Wynn." He pauses, but this time I'm dry eyed. "We don't think it was an accident—Barker was hit in the head." I stare at him and he continues. "We think maybe Barker got Parminder to agree to go for a walk, but almost immediately, Parminder must have found something to hit Barker with. The area was filled with banana trees. I don't know if you know how bananas grow, but dozens of bunches are on one low-hanging stalk. We think that's what Parminder used to kill Barker."

He has used the word I dreaded hearing. Barker was killed. But was she really killed by Parminder, or by her own foolishness?

"She was probably taken by surprise," he continues, "and fell. We think Parminder planned on driving away but then lost the car keys. Once she realized she couldn't drive, she must have taken her backpack and decided to walk instead. Probably she wanted to avoid the road so no one could see her. They found her body deep in the undergrowth. She must have tripped and fallen, and been unable to get up."

I don't really want to hear the details. Not of Parminder's death and not of Barker's. None of it makes any sense and I just let the words roll over me, trying not to think of what Barker's last moments must have been like, trying not to imagine Parminder's fear when Barker showed up. Maybe it really did happen the way

Detective Gordon says it did. Maybe Barker told Parminder she was going to force her to confess and that's why Parminder attacked Barker. That's the only part I really want to clarify.

"What makes you think Parminder attacked Barker? Couldn't it have been the other way around?" I ask.

Detective Gordon looks surprised by my question. "We don't think so. Parminder must have done it almost as soon as they started walking. Barker's body was barely ten yards from the car."

BARKER

CHAPTER THIRTY-TWO

On the short flight from Florida to Guatemala I order a vodka and tonic to calm my nerves and ask for extra peanuts which I eat one at a time, trying to steady my shaking hands. When I exit the airport, I pick up the rental car I booked online. The road out of the city is a reasonable two-lane highway but as I make my way into the hills, it narrows into a one-lane highway and then to being simply one lane. Every time there's a bend in the road, I'm terrified that a car will come whizzing around it and crash right into us. But I am the only one not used to driving these narrow, hairpin bends. The locals take it in stride, honking to let cars on my side of the bend know they're coming. In two hours, I have made it to a small village which is my signal to turn onto an unpaved road that goes into the hills. A few bumpy miles later, I see a small sign for the Proyecto Juvenil de la Paz, the Peace Youth Project.

The project is located on the side of a hill made green from the summer rain. I drive through a small wooden gate, and up a driveway lined with a profusion of wildflowers. It's even prettier than I remember it from fifteen years ago when I came and I am glad Parminder's last weeks were spent in such a beautiful place. There is no formal parking lot, so I park the car inside a grotto of banana trees where the profusion of vegetation hides it from sight. I can still remember the layout of the ranch and even though there are some new buildings now, the chapel is still in the same place. To one side of it is a separate cabana for the younger children who don't yet attend the Sunday morning mass, and as I hear American-accented Spanish wafting through the window, I know I've found my prey. I wait in silence for the activity to end. When it does, a rush of small children come tumbling out of the door, running toward the dining room across the pathway. Through the window, I see Parminder gather up their papers and straighten the little chairs back into a row, before finally exiting the room. I walk to the front of the building and grab her shoulder from behind. She spins around.

"What the—*Barker*? What are you doing here?" I can see she doesn't know whether to look pleased or concerned and that she's trying to keep that cool social worker look on her face to display no inappropriate emotion.

"You have to leave here Parminder, as soon as possible!" I tell her. "We have to go to your room and pack your stuff right away."

"What's going on?"

"It's Wynn. She's gone totally crazy. She's convinced that you framed her—I can't even begin to explain it all. Those girls you picked up were kidnapped and the police arrested her but she's certain you were behind it all."

Parminder nods her head. "Yes, I know. I spoke with her once by Skype. But what's that got to do with me leaving here?"

"Wynn's told everyone she can that you're the mastermind to the abduction. No one believes her of course, since we know it's not true. So now she's decided if no one will do anything, she has to do it herself. I told her I was going back to the retreat center so I could come and rescue you."

"But what does she want to do to me?" Parminder's voice is a little hesitant, but she's working hard to stay calm. Clearly, she thinks she could handle anything, even her ex-supervisor's paranoid lesbian partner.

"Crazy stuff. Last night she kept mumbling things about how she wanted to make you suffer. She used words like torture and murder…she wouldn't even tell me what her plan is."

"I don't understand. Why didn't you just get her committed to a mental hospital?"

"I tried, but in front of them, she appeared perfectly sane. I told them about the threats she'd made but she assured them that even though she's angry at you, she has no intention of harming you. They wouldn't keep her. I figured the best thing to do was to come here without her so I could get you away. Come on, there's no time to waste."

Finally, Parminder is convinced and we run quickly to her cabin. Luckily, she has traveled light and only has one large backpack into which she throws her things.

"I better go to the office and tell Señor Rodriguez what's happening," She says as she zips up the pack.

"No, don't leave any kind of trail. If she comes here, the less everyone knows the better. Write a note and say you had to leave unexpectedly and that you expect to be back within a few days." She complies, and then we head to the car.

I drive out of the gates, but instead of heading back to the city, I drive farther up the hill.

"Where are we going?" Parminder asks.

"We're going somewhere very safe, where it will be very hard to find you."

I keep driving, bumping along the muddy road. There are no other cars and I'm not surprised. When I was here years ago, I discovered this place, which even the locals didn't know about it. They said there were many overgrown areas that had paths leading to them, but most of them never got cultivated. The vegetation is so thick that it grows right to the edge of the track, so I can't park. I stop the car right where we are and we get out.

"Grab your backpack," I tell Parminder who is looking in wonder around her.

"What's behind the trees?" she asks as she heaves the backpack onto her back. "A house? A cabin? How on earth did you find out about it? It must be so well hidden."

She is her usual, annoying self, never giving me a chance to answer one question before she asks the next one. I wonder if I'm trying to dislike Parminder even more, so that I can deal better with what I'm about to do. We walk away from the dirt track, weaving through the tall Sapodillo trees and still there is nothing but dense vegetation. Beyond the trees that line the road, overgrown thickets of banana trees and twelve-foot-high bird of paradise crowd each other out.

I lead the way, pushing aside the massive leaves, the thick stalks already heavy with dangling bunches of unripe bananas as we force our way deeper into the growth. It starts to drizzle.

"Is it much farther?" she asks.

"Not too much," I say, because I can't quite decide how far to go. I thought I would just go a few minutes off the path, but each time I tell myself I've found the right place, I think I should go a bit farther. Parminder is breathing heavily from the exertion and so am I. I realize that the fact that she is wearing a backpack is an added stroke of luck for me in terms of what I have to do. The rain is falling steadily and it starts to get slippery. We plunge farther and farther into the undergrowth, while I keep telling myself, "You can do this, you must do this."

I told Wynn I was going back to the retreat center today and that tomorrow I would turn myself in to the police. Wynn sympathized and assured me we would hire a good lawyer so I could get a decent plea deal. But Wynn has always been naïve. First of all, we don't have money for a good lawyer. Secondly, I do not intend to ruin my life by going to prison or by losing my career.

As soon as she told me she knew what I'd done, I started brainstorming what I could do to change my plan. When she mentioned Parminder, I knew that was my answer. After we went to bed, she fell asleep instantly, but I was wide-awake, working the whole thing out before falling into a feverish sleep. I woke up so jittery yesterday morning that it took booking my flights and car, making an early morning run to the store, and taking a long walk with the dogs to calm me down. Thank goodness I never cancelled her mom's account with the debit card. Wynn thinks I took care of everything to do with her mom's finances, but for some reason, even back then, I figured it might be a good idea to hold onto this card. Now the rest of my plan is in motion. I already have Parminder's confession letter written up using the same lettering I used for the anonymous letters to Kallie's mom and the building manager. It's in the glove compartment of the car. I will mail it from Guatemala City directly to Detective Gordon. When he contacts me and tells me where the letter was mailed, I will remember that one of the places we discussed for a possible internship was the Peace Project just a couple of hours from the city. He will contact them and they'll tell him that she left very suddenly without telling anyone where she was going or why she was leaving. If he asks whether anyone was with her, they'll say they don't think so, because nobody saw us leave. Wynn will be off the hook and so will I. That is why I'm doing this, I remind myself and feel a sort of peace coming over me. I can really do this. I stop for a moment and ask Parminder to go in front.

"Oh," she says excitedly as she pulls ahead of me. "We're there?" My heart is racing as I reply.

"Yes," I say, and then I give Parminder the hardest push I can muster. She screams instinctively as the backpack makes her topple forward, face first into the undergrowth. As she sprawls on the ground facedown, I jump on her hips, making sure she can't move her legs. I lie on top of her and push the top of the pack down with all the force I can, so that it pushes her face into the ground. I don't know if she's trying to make any sounds because if she did, her mouth would quickly fill with mud and dirt. She struggles by flailing her arms up and down, but she can't grab me, nor can she get any traction because of the backpack on top of her. As I push down, I wonder at what point she started to feel scared, to realize that something awful was going on, but I can't let myself think about her feelings. Her arms scrabble and her legs kick, but her face is buried in wet leaves and she can't move. I press harder and harder.

It is only a matter of time before the flailing stops and I know that she has suffocated.

I stand up and pull myself off her body. I know that however annoying she was, she didn't deserve what I have done, but I had no choice. I choose Wynn above all others, and as a result, someone had to take the fall. I grin grimly to myself, thinking that that is exactly what she did. If they ever find her body, they will assume that she tripped and fell and suffocated in the mud. But I can't believe they will ever find her. I have chosen her spot well.

I look down at her, wondering whether I should say a prayer to whatever god she may have believed in. But the rain has become torrential and I have no time to waste. The sheets of rain are so heavy I can barely see in front of me. I wonder whether I should sit and wait it out, but I know that this may not just be an afternoon monsoon. It may go on for hours, or even days. I must make my way back to the car. I have a plane to catch in a few hours.

I push my way blindly forward, figuring that as long as I stay in a straight line, I should find myself back at the car within twenty minutes or so. The rain slows me down, but half an hour later I still haven't found the path. I decide to go back to Parminder's body so that I can start over. I turn around and as I walk, I picture my conversation with Detective Gordon.

"In the letter she says she's going to disappear so that no one can find her. Why would she have done that?"

"I think it may be because Wynn was hot on her trail. She tracked her down a couple of days ago."

"Why didn't she tell me?"

"She said the last time she tried to talk to you, you suggested that she was paranoid. She was still working on getting you more proof."

I will make Wynn a heroine.

"Her family members say there's no way she would just disappear. She's very close to them."

"Not really. She was desperate to get away from them. That's why she went to Guatemala instead of India."

"But I still don't understand her motive. She wanted to be a social worker and help people."

That is when I'll tell him that I had some very unsettling conversations with her in supervision. She was very judgmental about birth moms but since she was only a first-year student, I decided she should get another chance to see if she would become more professional in her second year.

I play the conversations repeatedly in my head to make sure I've left no stone unturned.

After forty minutes, I still haven't come across Parminder's body. By now, the earth beneath me is so saturated that pools of water are starting to form and I have to wade through them, or pick my way around them, further putting me off track. The sky is so black from the storm clouds pouring down rain that beneath the foliage, it is starting to get dark. My heart is racing as I feel the panic start to rise in me, as fast as the water is rising over the sodden fronds and leaves. I have to get out of here, but I don't know which way to go. The rain is still coming down in sheets and I can't see a thing. I push helplessly in all directions, wishing I'd left the car lights on to guide me, wishing I'd thought a bit more about how I would get back to the car, wishing I'd never started any of this. I think back to when I was at the airport looking at the TVs overhead. Did they mention a tropical storm? I don't know. I was so busy planning out everything that had to happen, that I didn't pay attention.

I have to get back to the car—but right now that seems to be impossible. I will have to stay here throughout the night and hope that in the morning, the sun comes out and the rain stops. I'll miss my flight, and will have some explaining to do to Wynn, but I'll figure something out.

I should never have confessed to Wynn. I should have insisted Parminder was making it all up. But for a moment it felt so good to finally unburden myself. Hopefully when she sees the signed confession from Parminder, I'll be able to persuade her that I was in some sort of psychosis and that most of what I told her wasn't true. I know she'll support me. She always does. We love each other. That's what love is. Supporting each other, no matter what.

The rain is so hard I can barely breathe. Every inch of me is a wet, sodden mess. I need to find a place to sit. If only I could climb a tree and sit on a sturdy branch, but banana trees and bird of paradise don't have trunks and branches like normal trees. I sit on the ground but immediately a pool of water starts to form around me. I'm shivering from cold.

For the first time I start to wonder what will happen if I don't make it out of here. What will become of Wynn? Everything I did was for her. I love her so much. I hope she knows that. I never meant to harm her, only to keep her safe. But now, I can't even keep myself safe. Like Parminder, I will drown, or suffocate, and no one will ever find me.

I have to get up. I have to get back to the car. I can't leave Wynn by herself. I pull myself out of the water and try to keep walking. Sharp edges from the fronds of the banana tree spike me and as I turn around, my head hits a low-hanging branch, and my knees buckle.

I feel myself sinking into the mud and starting to lose consciousness.

I know now that I will never hold Wynn again. I will never be able to tell her that everything I did today was for her. There will be no farewell letter expressing how much I loved her, and telling her that our years together were the happiest of my life.

There will only be silence.

EPILOGUE

Kallie, a year later

The judge is wearing a red robe. On the credenza is a picture of him with a middle-aged woman and two teenage boys. I guess they're his family. He sees me looking at the picture.

"It's good to be part of a family," he says. "You're going to find out just how good it is." He smiles at me, and I grin back. I've been trying not to look too soft, but today I just can't seem to stop smiling.

"Before we start, do you have any questions?" He looks at me and Mikki. She shakes her head. She looks serious, but I know underneath she's as happy as I am.

"How come you're wearing red? I thought judges always wore black."

"That's when we're in our courtroom. When I'm in my office, and especially when I'm presiding over a happy event, I like to wear my ceremonial robes."

"Why aren't we in court?" I ask, hoping I'm not being a smart-aleck. "I thought this was an official hearing."

"I think it's nicer for the families when I host you in my chambers. But don't worry, it's just as official when we do the paperwork here."

As long as it's official, that's all I care about.

I never thought this day would happen, and now that it's here, I can still hardly believe it. I don't know what happened to make Mom change her mind and agree to terminate her rights. She only has one more year in jail; she could've come out and started the whole family reunification thing again. That's what she's done a bunch of times. I thought it would just keep happening until I was eighteen, but something clicked for her this time. I don't know what it was.

"I know it's what's best for you," she told me on our last visit. "And I've always wanted that. I thought that by holding on to you, I was doing the right thing, trying to make it work. Now I see that all I was doing was standing in your way. Worse than that, I might have been setting you up to go down the same road I've traveled, and I'd do anything to prevent that." Mom's always contrite and sensible when she's off drugs. If only she could stay off them. "Don't think for a moment that I'm not sad to let you go, though." I can see in her eyes just how sad she is, but I can't let it sway me.

"I know," I told her. "Me too. My adoption worker says I could still see you if I want to, once you get out. She just thinks it's better if I take a break for now, while you're inside..."

Now here it is, adoption day. I wish Barker were here. But I guess I have the next best thing. If anyone would have told me I'd be adopted, I'd have bet my bottom dollar it would be Mrs. Clark who'd adopt us. But she's reunited with her own daughters (we didn't even know she had any!) and is working on building her relationship with them. She said she she hadn't been a good mom (which was hard to believe, but she assured us it was true.) By the time we were told about the adoption plan, we'd already started hanging out with our new mom, and it felt like an ideal match.

I was still sad about losing Mrs. Clark, but she said she'll always be our friend. I talked to my counselor about it—they made us go to counseling because they said that at the condo we'd been assaulted, and that we'd feel better if we talked about it. I told the counselor John was nice to us, but she said we were victims because he was so much older than us. The counselor kept using the word "trauma," but I guess she didn't get that when you've been in foster care for years, it takes a lot for you to feel traumatized. When I told her that, she said I was in denial. At that point I asked if I could drop out of counseling and Cindy, our new social worker, said I could. I think Mikki still goes though.

So now we're here, in the judge's chambers. Evie and Dot are standing at the back of the room, along with Mrs. Clark and her daughters. I wish Barker was here. I miss her.

Wynn is wearing a flowery top and purple pants. She has bangles up and down her arms. She's cool. I asked her if I have to call her Mom but she said I can call her whatever I want. We don't live in the house she and Barker had. She said it held too many memories but I think she sold it so she could afford to adopt us and still keep doing her jewelry. I've helped her set up an online business and she said she makes much more money than she ever did before. I don't think we were supposed to know about the financial stuff but one day I overheard Wynn telling Evie on the phone that she gets adoption assistance because we're considered 'special needs.' I bolted in there and started yelling, "What do you mean we're special needs? I'm not some kid who's disabled or has a mental disorder!"

"No, you're not. But you're special to me," she said, giving me a hug. "Any child who's over the age of eight when they're adopted is considered special needs. It's a good thing, because it means the state gives me money to look after you, which will pay for tennis and swimming and all those cargo shorts you buy!"

When we first moved in, Wynn told us that sometimes she's a bit forgetful and absent-minded. She said if we want to be sure she's listening to us, we have to ask her to stop what she's doing and say directly, "Wynn, I need you to hear this." It feels weird to do that, but it seems to work, because she's remembered everything I need her to, like when we have to take cupcakes to school.

Wynn's generally a pretty happy person. Occasionally I catch her staring into space and I figure she must be thinking about Barker. When she sees me watching her, she shakes her head as if pulling herself away from something she doesn't want to think about and stretches her arms above her, as if she's just said a little prayer to the universe.

I like that I can talk about myself with her. I'm getting more used to the idea of being gay, but it helps to know that she was with boys for a while and can relate to that side of things. Wynn told us she was adopted too. Not like us, she said she was much younger. She said her mom gave her up, like our moms had to, and that for the longest time she always felt inferior because of it.

"How long did it take you to feel as good as everyone else?" I asked and she laughed and said that to tell the truth, she's still working on that.

After Wynn signs the papers, the judge says that because we're sixteen, he'd like us to sign them too.

"I need to know that you are doing this of your own free will and that it is what you want." We assure him it is, and I sign as quickly as possible, so no one can change their minds.

Wynn asked us earlier whether we wanted to go out for dinner to celebrate, or whether we wanted her to make our favorite foods. I don't like going to fancy restaurants because then I have to dress up and I'd much rather wear cargo shorts whenever I can, so I opted for staying at home. Mikki made a face because she's really into dresses and girly things, so we compromised. Tonight Wynn's cooking for everyone at home, and tomorrow Evie and Dot are taking Mikki to a real fancy restaurant where she can glam up as much as she wants.

When we leave the judge's chambers, the sun is shining high in the sky.

"What a beautiful day," Wynn says, smiling.

I couldn't agree more.

THE END

IF YOU ENJOYED THIS BOOK…

Reviews are like giving a tip when you received good service. Positive online reviews make an enormous difference to writers. If you enjoyed this novel, please consider placing a review (a simple one-liner is fine!) on Amazon, Goodreads, Twitter, your Facebook page, and anywhere else where people might see it.

ALSO BY ALISON R. SOLOMON

Devoted

Ashley Glynn knows there's more to her sister's untimely death than meets the eye. But as she investigates, Ashley is forced to confront the deep conflict within her own life between long-held religious beliefs and her sexuality. How can she discover the truth about her sister's death, if she can't face the truth about her own life?

Wild Girl Press, 2017
ISBN (Print) 978-0-9984400-0-2

Timing Is Everything

A hit-and-run.
A terrified suspect.
A woman caught between her friend and her lover.

Wynn Larimer is putting out the trash late one night when a car smashes into her, injuring her so badly that her entire livelihood is put in jeopardy. The accused perpetrator is Gabriella Luna. The timing couldn't be worse—Gabriella is about to become a permanent resident but is now terrified of being deported. Caught in the middle of it all is Kat Ayalon, who is Wynn's best friend but in love with Gordy. How can Kat support both women, if helping one means selling out the other?

Wild Girl Press, 2018
ISBN (Print) 978-9984400-2-6

ABOUT THE AUTHOR

Alison R. Solomon grew up in England, and lived in Israel and Mexico before settling in the USA. *Along Came the Rain*, was her debut novel. Her most recent novel, *Timing is Everything*, won Best of the Bay, 2018. Her short stories have been published in anthologies and magazines in the USA and Mexico. When she's not writing or providing social work consulting services, Alison can be found playing tennis or planning a trip. She lives with her wife and two rescue dogs in Gulfport, Florida.

Keep up on Alison's latest news and projects or join her newsletter at: www.AlisonRSolomon.com

www.ingramcontent.com/pod-product-compliance
Lightning Source LLC
Chambersburg PA
CBHW020906180626
46816CB00007BA/2271